Druid's Croft & Other Short Stories by AM Burrage

Alfred McLelland Burrage was born in Hillingdon, Middlesex on 1st July, 1889. His father and uncle were both writers, primarily of boy's fiction, and by age 16 AM Burrage had joined them. The young man had ambitions to write for the adult market too. The money was better and so was his writing.

From 1890 to 1914, prior to the mainstream appeal of cinema and radio the printed word, mainly in magazines, was the foremost mass entertainment. AM Burrage quickly became a master of the market publishing his stories regularly across a number of publications. By the start of the Great War Burrage was well established but in 1916 he was conscripted to fight on the Western Front. He continued to write during these years documenting his experiences in the classic book War is War by Ex-Private X.

For the remainder of his life Burrage was rarely printed in book form but continued to write and be published on a prodigious scale in magazines and newspapers. In this volume we concentrate on his supernatural stories which are, by common consent, some of the best ever written. Succinct yet full of character each reveals a twist and a flavour that is unsettling.....sometimes menacing....always disturbing.

There are many other volumes available in this series together with a number of audiobooks. All are available from iTunes, Amazon and other fine digital stores.

Table Of Contents

Druid's Croft

In order to discover the exact date when this highly unusual and very unpleasant adventure befell Clive Radlett I should have, strangely enough, to consult "Ruff's Guide." I know that it happened in the April of a recent year. Those who are interested in a detail which, after all, is not essential, may time it to the hour by discovering for themselves the date of Dry Mat's victory in the City and Suburban.

You know Clive Radlett's work? They say in the little studios where moneymaking is regarded as a crime against art that popularity has killed whatever mediocre gifts he may once have had. They say that he is over lavish with colour but otherwise too photographic. But there is no denying his popularity, and to call an artist popular is to pronounce his artistic damnation. There may or may not be a little jealousy. One can never be quite sure.

Mr. Charles J. Bungey, at least, was blind to whatever demerits the artistic eye might have detected in Radlett's work. He had already bought three of Radlett's landscapes at an exhibition in New York. When he paid his first visit to England Radlett was the man he sought and found.

Mr. Bungey came of English descent, and had discovered, by dint of long and tedious inquiries, that the fertile acres of Hampshire had enriched the blood of his forefathers. Sometime in the middle of the eighteenth century a George Bungey had run away from a farm on the edge of the New Forest and crossed the seas to help lay the foundations of a great new country. From this George Bungey was Charles J. indisputably descended. The New Forest district of Hampshire, therefore, became his second home, by a mental process of adoption.

He was not a millionaire, but well-to-do, even for an American. At least, he 'could afford to indulge a whim which prompted him to take back half a dozen pictures of the New Forest and point them out to his friends as representing the "I'ilole spot" from which his ancestors sprang. Immediately he thought of Radlett. Never were skies more vividly blue, nor trees a richer green, nor heather a more slumbrous purple than in Radlett's pictures. So he got an introduction to the painter and offered him a commission.

"I'd be obliged if you'd go down and paint the New Forest for me, Mr. Radlett," he said, much as he might have asked an inferior kind of craftsman to distemper a room. He named a sum of money much in excess of Radlett's expectations. So Radlett went.

The work seemed likely to occupy Radlett from early spring until the end of summer. It was therefore desirable that Radlett should find for himself a furnished house in, or in the near neighbourhood of, the Forest. Although he was a single man living alone, save for the married couple who cooked, cleaned, and valeted for him, he did not want too small a house. In his poorer days he had had too much acquaintanceship with "desirable cottage residences" of the type which are supposed to—and do—attract artists. He knew all their inconveniences, from the beams against which the unwary constantly banged their heads to the water from the well outside the back door, in which life was visible even to the naked eye. He liked space, and he could afford it at last. In this three-dimensioned existence one can only be present in one room at the same time, but Radlett liked to think that there were twenty other rooms at his disposal.

When Radlett saw Druid's Croft advertised in a Sunday paper as a house to be let furnished for three months or longer, he assumed that it would be too expensive for him. There were fourteen bedrooms. Mention was made of three tennis courts, large flower and vegetable gardens, and "grounds comprising twenty acres in all." Obviously it was a small mansion, and probably a rent commensurate with its size would be demanded for it. But he eyed the advertisement wistfully, because it made mention of a studio. Most of his painting would be done out of doors, but he would need a room with a good north light for such work as he would be able to do indoors. However, the advertisement concluded with the names of the local agents, and it occurred to him that they must have other houses on their books, and were therefore worth a visit.

Accordingly Radlett rose early one morning, got out his car, and drove just under a hundred miles into the little town of Broddington, to interview Messrs. Everest & Millby, auctioneers, surveyors, and estate agents. He arrived shortly before noon on the morning of the day that Dry Mat enriched most bookmakers and a very few of the general public by winning the City and Suburban at the pleasing odds of thirty-three to one.

The living representatives of Messrs. Everest & Millby go by names which are of no importance to the story. There has been no Millby within living memory. The late Mr. Everest, deeply committed in Consols, died of anxiety while awaiting the result of the battle, of Waterloo. Having walked into the office and asked to see one or the other of them, Radlett received a bright smile from a genial young clerk who said that both the partners were out and could he be of any service?

Radlett stated his requirements. The young clerk took down a ledger of such dimensions that it might have stood in the offices of the Recording Angel and been labelled "Nero." He turned over several pages, seemingly at random, and then looked up with an inspired smile.

"Of course," he said, "there's Druid's Croft."

"Yes," said Radlett, "I saw the advertisement, and that's what brought me here. But I think that house is going to be beyond my means. This part of the world isn't too cheap in the summer."

"How much do you want to run to, sir?"

"As little as I can. How much is Druid's Croft? "

"Ten guineas a week."

Radlett stared.

I thought you were going to say twenty or thirty. I don't at all mind ten guineas a week. But what's the snag? "

The clerk tapped his fingers on the desk, and then examined his nails. Obviously he was trying to invent phrases.

"Well, sir, the furniture isn't too good. It's a good house, but it isn't what you'd call a posh place inside. The owner's in India, and he wants to sell it—at his own price—so naturally he won't have new furniture put in. Our instructions are to let it furnished, if we can, while we're finding a purchaser. I don't mean to say that it's uncomfortable; but things are a bit falling to pieces, and people who want to take a big place furnished generally expect to find everything about it just so."

Radlett smiled.

"I think," he said, "that this is going to be the house of my dreams. I have had some experience of furnished houses, and it would be a refreshing change not to be accused of doing ten pounds worth of damage every time a castor falls, off a chair."

The other laughed.

"You couldn't do ten pounds' worth of damage in that house, not unless you took a box of Mills' bombs with you. I don't mean that the furniture and decorations are impossible to live with, but everything's just a bit worn out and shabby. That makes just the difference when it comes to letting a place furnished."

"I'd like to see it," said Radlett. "Is there a caretaker there?"

"No; there's an old woman who comes in twice a week and keeps the place aired. You'll find the beds O.K. But I don't guarantee you'll find her, so if you'd like to see the house I'll send for the keys.'

An office boy was sent in search of them. The interim was one of those gulfs which are most easily bridged by genial chatter.

Radlett was popular with all clashes and grades of human beings. He had a merry eye. Strangers addressed him with confidence. Servants liked him. Wealthy patrons shed: pomposity and put on humanity when talking to him. He had a natural gift for appearing— and being— the kind of man who can be talked to; and he could talk on most subjects. The clerk appraised him.

"Well, sir," he said suddenly, "what's going to win the big race this afternoon?"

Radlett's eyes smiled. Racing was one of his hobbies. He was a good judge of horseflesh and of form, and he had friends from whom he received "information" which was not invariably false. Whether on the aggregate he won or lost a little money on the Turf was a matter for conjecture to a. man who hated keeping accounts; but if he lost he did not lose much.

"I think the favourite, Star of Troy, will about win," he said. "But if you want an outsider, I hear Dibley is very keen about the chances of Dry Hat. I've had a small saver on it. Not a bad little handicapper, nicely weighted, and Monson up. Won over the same course last year, but hadn't much to beat. He was thirty-three to one this morning, and I don't suppose the S.P. will be much less. Must have a sort of chance if Dibley seriously fancies him. At any rate, I think he's worth a nibble."

"Thanks, sir," said the clerk, "I'll nibble."

A minute or two later the keys were brought, and Radlett, having been told exactly where to find the house, drove himself away in that direction.

The gates leading to Druid's Croft stood on the very margin of a tract of the Forest, with only a narrow road faced with loose yellow gravel between them and a gently undulating heath which rolled on to meet a line-of trees standing up blue and misty on the horizon. The house itself was of red brick, and it had been built in the middle of Queen Victoria's reign when architecture was at its worst. However, its designer had not indulged the then prevailing passion for serrated battlements, absurd little turrets, and all the trivial eyesores beloved of his contemporaries.

Radlett drove himself round to the front door steps, got out of the car, and let himself into the house. Within a few minutes he became aware that all that the clerk had told him about the interior of the house was true. The furniture was old without being, in the phrase of the dealers, antique. It belonged to the worst Victorian period. The mahogany frameworks of chairs and sofas might endure for ever, but the upholsteries and curtains were in a sad condition.

"Good house for a blind man to live in," thought Radlett.

Everywhere his sensitive nose detected faint odours of dust and decay, although the rooms were clean and cared for. It was as if the house were a living and mortal thing, suffering from some incurable malady. Myriads of invisible and inaudible animalcule were at work on the slow process of destruction. Radlett snuffed the atmosphere and found it not to his liking. Still, the studio was most important. He went to find the studio.

Here he was agreeably disappointed. The studio was comparative modern, an annexe to the house built next to the servants' hall. It was healthy. There was no mouldy upholstery or hangings, and little furniture of any sort: just a few plain chairs and a grand piano. Obviously it had been the studio of a musician and not of a painter. Still, the north light was there. He walked over, tried the piano, and winced at the sounds it produced. It seemed not to have been touched, much less tuned, within twenty years. Well, that did not matter. The north light was there, and there was nothing to offend the eye.

The rooms upstairs, whither he next made his way, were much as lie might have expected—large enough and in a state of not quite unendurable dilapidation. No wonder Druid's Croft was to be let furnished—if it could be so called—at a rental of ten guineas a week. Still, could he do better elsewhere? There, was the house's position right on the edge of the Forest, and the excellent studio, to be considered. Moreover, it was a house in which accidents and breakages could bring him to no great financial grief. On his way downstairs he was more than half persuaded to take it.

He re-entered the mouldering drawing-room, and there the strange, disturbing thing befell him. Let us take the story from his own lips as he told it half an hour later in the consulting-room of Dr. Stanley's house in Bridlington.

"I've had a seizure or something," Radlett explained rather breathlessly. "Nothing like it's ever happened to me before."

"Eh?" The doctor picked up a wrist, held it for a moment, and then went to fetch a stethoscope. He listened gravely for a while. "Now," he said, "we'll try the blood pressure."

When this had been done he smiled a wan professional smile.

"No," he said, "you haven't had a stroke, but you seem to have excited yourself a great deal about something. Now tell me what happened."

"We'll, to begin with, I was struck blind for the space of a few minutes."

"Blind?"

"Yes. Quite literally blind. I was looking over a furnished house I think of taking, and I was standing in the drawing-room when the thing came upon me. But that isn't all. I was seized with the most intense, the most murderous, hatred for some thing or somebody which I supposed to be upstairs, although I should have known that the house was empty. I had only been over the house once, but I felt my way upstairs, goaded by a dreadful lust for killing, although I was still as blind as a man born without eyes. I can't remember precisely what happened after that. The darkness came over my mind as well. But when light and reason came back to me I found myself bending over the bed in the best room, with a pillow between my clenched hands, shaking it as a terrier shakes a rat. I just stood aghast at myself and then came away. What do you make of it, Dr. Stanley? Do you think I am going mad?"

The doctor smiled.

"I should say not. What house was this, may I ask?"

"Druid's Croft."

"Druid's Croft. Yes, I know. H'm!" He looked thoughtful for a moment. "Well, in my opinion you've had what in the language of laymen is called a nerve storm. You're Mr. Radlett, the painter, are you not? I've had a little experience of men with temperaments. You've nothing to fear. I can give you a prescription for a tonic, if you like; "but you would perhaps prefer to consult your own medical man when you return, to Town."

Radlett heaved a sigh of relief. In his opinion all doctors were the same.

"Oh, I'll take your prescription, thanks," he said.

Dr. Stanley turned to his desk and began to write those strange hieroglyphics which are understood only by chemists. And while he wrote he spoke.

"Perhaps this part of the world doesn't suit you. I should think twice about staying here if I were you."

"I must. I've work to do."

"Then—er—Druid's Croft. Rather mouldy and depressing, isn't it? Wouldn't you be more comfortable in a bright modern house?"

"If I can find one with a studio, but I don't think I can."

Dr. Stanley gave, him the prescription and a smile.

"Well," he said, "I've given you my advice. If you take Druid's Croft and have any more trouble come and see me again. I think you'd be the better for brighter and more cheerful surroundings."

"Oh, I shall be out of doors most of the time," Radlett assured him.

HE paid the modest sum demanded and drove on to the house agent, where the clerk who had previously received him wore the smile of Alice's Cheshire Cat.

"I don't know how to thank you, sir," he blurted out. "It's been a godsend to me. I hope you had a good win."

"Eh?" said Radlett.

"Haven't you heard, sir? Dry Mat won the City at thirty-threes."

"Did he?" Radlett smiled faintly.

"Well, as I told you, he wasn't my first choice, but I haven't had a bad race."

"I've had a good one, thanks to you. Tell you the truth, sir, I was in a bit of a mess. I'm a married man, and I was in a bit of debt and—well, things were looking a bit desperate. No good me backing favourites. So, I had two pounds on Dry Mat, and won sixty-six, and now: I'm out of all my troubles, thanks to you."

Radlett stared at him.

"Young man," he said, "don't you ever do that again. If your own brother, much more a stranger, gives you a racing tip, thank him kindly and keep your money in your pocket. This may never happen again."

"I know, sir. Oh, you can trust me. I've had my lesson. Only, you see, I was desperate. Two pounds didn't matter in the state I was in."

"Well, all's well that ends well. I've been over Druid's Croft, and I've decided to take it for three months. Would it be convenient for somebody to go through the inventory with me on Monday next?"

The young man leaned over and dropped his voice.

"Excuse me, sir. You've done me a bit of good and I should like to do a bit of good for you. But you see what my position is here. I shouldn't be here long if anybody knew I'd dropped you a hint. You spend a night in Druid's Croft before you decide to take it. I can't tell you why. You've got the keys. Don't hand them in here until to-morrow. You'll find the beds aired. There's an old woman who comes in and looks after the place. I know her, and I'll make it right with her so that she doesn't let on about you staying there. But you have a night there before you put pen to paper."

There was something portentously serious about the young man, and Radlett stared.

"What's all this about?" he asked.

"I can't tell you, sir. And if I did you wouldn't listen. But I'm giving you a tip —as good a tip as you gave me. Oh, and, sir, it might be advisable for you to buy a local guide-book. You can get one at Murland's next door."

Radlett was frankly puzzled. There seemed to be a local prejudice against Druid's Croft.

"Well," he admitted, "I certainly had a very queer turn there this afternoon, but it couldn't have had anything to do with the house."

"You had something happen to you? Well, some people do—especially artistic gentlemen like yourself. And you still want to take it! Well, sir, take my advice and keep the keys until to-morrow morning."

Radlett considered. We are not concerned with any vague thoughts which may have been revolving in his mind.

"Yes," he said slowly, "I think I will, thank you."

The clerk looked relieved.

"And you won't forget the guide-book, sir?"

"I won't, It's bound to be useful to me when I come down here. I'll buy one as I go out. Good afternoon and thank you."

Radlett bought the guide-book, slipped it into his pocket, and prepared to spend the rest of the day and the night in Broddington. Truth to tell, he was not sorry to give himself an excuse for remaining. It would be a terrible thing if he suffered a recurrence of what had happened during the afternoon while he was driving his car. He had the prescription made up and savoured the familiar flavour of a strong tonic containing the usual ingredients which are supposed to restore shattered nerves.

He passed what remained of the afternoon and the early evening in examining the few places of interest of which the town could boast, and at seven o'clock he dined at the Crown and remained there for as long as the law would allow him, which was until ten. As the time passed he found himself curiously unwilling to revisit Druid's Croft. Once bitten twice shy. Yet he had been willing to take the house for three months. The few words uttered by the young man at the office had already half succeeded in foisting him off his original intention. What was the reason for begging him to spend a night there before committing himself? Obviously because he was likely to suffer some unpleasant experience which might deter him from paying in advance for the use of an uninhabitable house. It was all vague and not very reassuring. Was, after all, the atmosphere of the house in some way responsible for his strange "seizure" of the afternoon?

At ten o'clock he drove his car round to Druid's Croft and left it on the drive outside the front door. It was as well he did this, for he needed it in a hurry.

Having let himself in he discovered, of course, that the electric light was not working, a contingency against which he had come unprepared. However, he found his way upstairs with the aid of matches, and entered the best bedroom. He was not fond of that room—it was where blindness and an unreasonable hate had led him that afternoon—but he was still less fond of a damp bed. It occurred to him that if the old woman who came in to look after the house were inclined to scamp her work this was the bed least likely to have been neglected. He partly undressed and got between the sheets, not without a faint sense of repulsion. But after a while he fell into a troubled sleep, from which he wakened suddenly for no reason that he was able to name.

He sat up and listened and his heart began to thump. Undoubtedly he was not alone in the house. Somebody was coming upstairs. He tried to calm the horror which quickened his pulses to a gallop. It could only be some tramp who knew the house and had come for a night's shelter. Yet how had he got in? Radlett remembered bolting the front door behind him, and all the other doors were locked and barred.

'The halting footfalls reached the landing and turned in the direction of his room. He heard the soft drumming of a hand fumbling its way along the outside of the wall. Then the door opened, and Radlett hardly checked himself from screaming like a child.

That which entered was in the form of a man, but its hair was long. Its cruel, working, distorted face was the colour of death. The hands with long fingers fumbled and clutched; and it was through these gestures that the truth first penetrated to Radlett's tortured brain that the' visitant was blind.

One clutching hand found the corner of the chest of drawers, and this immediately seemed to give to the intruder the direction of the bed. It came with outflung hands towards Radlett, who screamed aloud and sprang out of the bed on the far side. Even as he fled from the room he was aware of the thing bending over the bed and snarling and worrying, even as he had snarled and worried over it during his strange aberration of the afternoon.

If you can get the Boots at the Crown totalk, he will tell you a story which he thinks is amusing, about how he was knocked up at two in the morning by a gentleman who arrived in a car which he had driven in his underclothes.

The visitor's rather weak explanation was that his outer garments had been stolen by a tramp while he had gone for a midnight swim in the river. You will also learn how the gentleman had to stay in bed next morning until the local outfitter came round with some ready-made clothes in which he was able to depart.

Radlett had lost the guide-book he had bought, having left it in his coat pocket, but he found another in his bedroom, and he read it in the morning while he was awaiting the arrival of the outfitter. He came, across- the following passage:

"Passing on the left Druid's Croft, a house of sortie morbid interest as having been the country home of Pirensky and the scene of the tragedy. It will be remembered how, some thirty years ago, Pirensky, the blind pianist, strangled his wife in a fit of jealousy."

Radlett threw the book on to the floor. He did not want to read further.

Druid's Croft is still to be let furnished, or to be sold. The sum asked for it is not high. But it is one of those houses which would be dear at any price.

A CASTLE FAIR
I built a castle, grand and high,
Whose corner stone was gold;
With parapets adorned with gems,
A wonder to behold.
A monument to me, I thought,
Which there shall always stay,
But when misfortune's winds did blow,
'Twas wrecked, and swept away.

Another castle reared I then,
Upon the rock of fame,
That things which I had said and done,
Might set the world aflame.
But white the passing years were few,
That castle, too, came down,
For others, soon, of greater deeds,
Arose to claim renown.

Undaunted, wiser than of old,
I builded yet once more,
And raised a castle, fair to see,
Quite different from before.
Though storms and trials of life assail,

And clouds are black above,
That castle stands, and will for e'er,
For it is built of love.

The Wardrobe, A Ghost Story

It was Mason himself who showed me to my room. So glad were he and Philippa to see me, and so glad was I to see them, and so much did we find necessary to chatter about immediately, that a full hour had elapsed since the ancient car from the village station brought me to their door.

Mason was one of my oldest friends, and I had known Philippa before she became his wife; but this was my first visit to Greybarrow, for the reason that Mason had only just acquired it.

It was just the sort of house I should have expected him to possess. He was a poor man who loved space and elbow-room, and swore that he stifled in rooms of an ordinary size. Greybarrow was square and ugly and pretentious on the outside; inside it was roomy enough in all conscience, and sparsely furnished, and would have seemed comfortless if any but the Masons had inhabited it. But there was something about these two good, cheerful friends of mine that would have made any abode seem habitable.

Cecil Mason was a literary man—I had almost written hack. He wrote biographies, nature notes, articles on bric-a-brac; indeed he seemed to have chosen all the most poorly paid branches of his profession. But he had been guilty of a "costume" drama, a vile Wardour-Street production, which had run for a hundred and fifty nights in a West End theatre, and made possible his marriage and the purchase of Greybarrow. Greybarrow was under-staffed and poorly furnished, but Mason had the high-ceilinged rooms for which his soul had yearned, his elbow-room, his books and his wife.

We passed the first storey, and a little to my surprise he preceded me up a second staircase.

"You don't mind being taken a little nearer to Heaven?" he asked over his shoulder. "We've given you a room on the top floor for two reasons. One of them is that it's the finest room in the house."

"And the other?" I asked.

"Oh, you'll see that in a moment."

The room into which he presently led me was enormous. I think a wall must have been knocked down by some former owner, thus turning two good-sized rooms into one. I know that the little iron single bedstead with its cretonne eiderdown quilt looked ridiculous by reason of the space around it.

But what took my eye and immediately took my interest was the largest oak wardrobe I had ever seen in my life. It was a monstrous piece of furniture, and it made the little bed and the little wash-hand-stand look all the more dwarfed, like articles of doll-house furniture. The wardrobe almost exactly fitted the whole range of wall fronting the bed. Its top reached to within an inch or two of the ceiling, and there was no room for a man to press himself around either of its sides. There were four doors to it, each as large as the front entrance to a small villa.

"That's the other reason why we've given you this room," said Mason, seeing the direction in which my gaze was turned. "This is the best piece of furniture in the house, and this is the only room that can accommodate it."

"I don't wonder at it," I remarked. "Where on earth did you get it?"

"I bought it cheap," said Mason, and we both laughed. Such an unwieldy piece of furniture would have to be cheap indeed before most men would buy it.

"Halstead," he continued, "a neighbour of mine over at the Grange, bought it at a sale at Chilby Hall, about ten miles away. When it arrived he found that it wouldn't go into any of his rooms, and he was faced by the alternative of getting rid of it cheaply and quickly or breaking it up for firewood. Knowing that I had one or two big rooms here, he came rushing over to me, and sold it to me at a substantial Joss."

While he was speaking he threw open one of the doors.

"There are no partitions inside," he added. "Look."

I looked inside and down the dim length of it. There were rows of hooks along the back, and more hooks depended front the great oak beams close to its top.

"I wonder," I remarked, "who could have caused such a monster to be made."

Mason opened the other doom.

"Some eighteenth-century blood," he arid. "It is as old as that. Some fellow who loved clothes, and liked to see the best of his beautiful raiment all at once. It must have looked a sight, too, if you can imagine his coats and waistcoats and breeches. At least, that's how I think it came to be constructed. It was a rare pantomime. I can tell you, getting it up the stairs and placing it here. Well, old man, do you think you'll be comfortable?"

"Of course I shall," I laughed. "That piece of furniture is a bit overwhelming, but I should feel honoured at being allowed to hang my coat in it."

Five minutes later I was downstairs and having tea, and had forgotten all about the wardrobe; and it was not until I went up to prepare for dinner that I remembered it again. As I hung up my discarded clothes in that enormous interior I felt much as a beggar might feel who bad lodged himself in a dual palace in some deserted town.

I hope, my friend," I remarked to the giant as I changed, "that you're not going to creak all night."

I faced it again shortly after eleven o'clock when I came up candle in hand, while Mason called the last good-nights to me from the landing below. In the dim light the great piece of furniture seemed larger and bulkier than ever. Had its upper panels been of glass, it would have looked irresistibly like a railway carriage shorn of its wheels. As it was, it gave me to think of some absurdly sumptuous cattle truck. I opened one of the inner doors and hung up my evening clothes and my dressing-gown before blowing out the candle and getting into bed.

My blind was up and my window open, but little light invaded the room, for the night was cloudy and moonless. Rut in the dim illumination of the night skies, which focussed tiny gleams upon the bed rail, I could make out the shape of the great wardrobe, the outlines of its four doors, and the glint of its brass knobs. From where I lay, with my eyes but two or three feet above the flow level, the great wardrobe seemed taller and more enormous than ever. It seemed to lean down on me, as if arrested and held in the act of falling. Its size and slope obsessed and oppressed me; there was something about it I did not like. It wet an absurdity, but it was a sinister absurdity. After a little while, however, I turned on my side, and presently, unawares, dropped off to sleep. I was tired after my journey, and the excitement of seeing the Masons and talking over old times had used up more of my nervous force than I had imagined. But I had slept for only about an hour when I dreamed that I was being strangled.

There was no dream except the mere fact of strangulation. There was something vice-like about my throat which robbed me of the power to breathe. I writhed this way and that in an agony of terror and physical suffering. Strangely enough, I knew quite well that I was asleep, and amidst the galloping stampede of terrors which thundered in my head I prayed for some merciful chance to wake me.

Something did wake me. I did not know what it was at the time, but my eyes opened and the numbness which had chained my limbs suddenly left them. I sat up open-eyed, and awake, and still for one ghastly moment I could not breathe. Then breath returned, and I drank the air in, one lung, choking gasp as I sprang out of bed.

I could still feel the tightness of the throat, but that departed as I breathed and breathed. My heart was pounding as it I had just been running for my life, I was throbbing and trembling in every part of my body. I staggered to the wash hand-stand and gulped down some water.

In a minute or two I was better, hut although I was no hypochondriac, I was seriously alarmed. I had never before had such a seizure, nor could I guess the cause of it. It was no mere nightmare, nor could I put it down to indigestion.

On my way back to bed I discovered at least the cause of my sudden waking. One of the doors of the wardrobe had sprung ajar, and the rasping dick of its latch had called me back to life from that vile death struggle which had been forced upon me in my sleep. I closed the door and tried the brass knob. It seemed firm enough. Ordinarily I should have wondered a great deal at a door with so stable a latch having opened of itself, but just then I had other things to think of.

Back in bed, I wooed sleep cautiously, as if she were a perfidious lover in whose arms treachery might await me. I had already had that night one experience of her caresses. But now, apart from the disturbances in my mind, there were outside influences to keep me awake. Accentuated by the complete stillness of the room and of the world outside, the wardrobe became a centre of quiet activity. Behind its doors—so I received the impression—something was moving, and these movements, silent for the most part, culminated from time to time in little hushed noises, the creaking of a beam or a sudden knock as of an elbow striking the panels. And presently came a succession of shuffling sounds, as of somebody groping about inside.

My heart, which had slowly resumed its normal measure since my waking, began once more to flog my ribs. Uneasiness had turned to sudden alarm. I sat there quite still and heard the blood singing in my ears like a distant sound of the sea. And then, while my strained attention would have made the least sound to break explosively in my ears, with a sudden snap, which sounded like the crack of a pistol, one of the wardrobe doors sprang open.

My whole body seemed to jerk as if, in the act of hurrying, I had caught my sleeve upon a nail. Then I gathered ray wits and tried to laugh at myself. There was no doubt that I was ill. That hideous dream of being strangled was sufficient proof. And now sickness assailed me in the form of childish terrors of the dark. In the daytime one takes no notice of creaking furniture, or the springing open of a door, the scampering of mice behind a wainscot, yet these intruders, scarcely strong enough to break the web of a flimsy thought by day, can masquerade terribly under the cloak of night. Summoning reason to my aid, I climbed out of bed.

It was not the same door of the wardrobe which had previously sprung open. This time it was the end door on the left. I dosed it and tried its latch. Again the latch seemed firm enough, although I tried it only once. I will own that I approached that wardrobe with a sense of fear, of nausea, which no reasoning on my part could eliminate. I fumbled with the brass knob of the door with a sort of breathless dread, and then sprang hastily back from it, as if I were in contact with something likely at any moment to explode.

Back in bed, I contemplated re-lighting my candle and striving to soothe my nerves by reading from one of the books left handily on a small table beside me; but I turned from the thought as pandering to something in me which was alike childish and cowardly.

Meanwhile, strive as I would, I could not rid myself of the impression that the doors of the wardrobe masked from my gaze some stealthy, nameless activities which were going on within the silence - faint shufflings, little creakings as if of wood complaining under a burden, sharp cracks, and more than once something which sounded like a football. And suddenly again I was forced out of bed, for another door sprang open.

The saner side of myself discovered a reason for this sudden bursting open of the doors, and if I could theorise less comfortably than in the daytime on the expanding and contracting of timber and the effect upon it of a range of weather I could at least chance at that life-line and save myself from complete nervous collapse. I was determine to put an end to at least part of these disturbances, and was half-way out of bed with the intention of throwing wide open all the doors, when I realised that I could not bear to lie in bed with nothing between me and the and the interior of that wardrobe, in which my clothes, hanging there, would take grotesque, half-human shapes. But fortunately there was a chair in the room for every door, I closed the door which had sprung open and backed a chair against it. I carried chairs to each of the three other doors, trembling with a reasonless anguish of the mind each time I approached that massive piece of furniture. Then I returned to bed and buried my head among the clothes.

There, with my hearing muffled, I could still catch faint sounds from beyond the foot of my bed. There was one which sounded like a faint groan, and I broke out into a profuse sweat as I lay in an agony of apprehension lest it should be repeated. But sleep come mercifully to me at last, and ended only in broad sunlight with a knock on my door and a voice outside announcing the arrival of a cup of tea, and enquiring when I would take my bath.

I did not feel at my best, but the fears of the night were gone—gone until I got out of bed and saw what had happened during my last sleep. Three of the wardrobe doors stood ajar, the chairs having been pushed back an inch or two. The fourth door was open wide, and the chair, which had failed to keep it closed, had been flung half a dozen paces and lay as nearly upside down as a chair will balance, close to the foot of my bed.

I stared at it as roundly and as amazedly as if I had actually seen it move. Here was something which, baffled all reason. The chair was no flimsy trifle: it was a stout piece of mahogany. Even allowing for the fact that my head was beneath the blankets, I must have been sunk in a deep sleep not to have heard the crash of it over-turning. No mere expansion or contraction of timber such as might cause a door to spring open could account for this. Yet with the blessed sunlight around me warning the carpet under my bare feet I was sure that something governed by the normal laws was responsible for it.

Over breakfast I told the Masons, and they both laughed.

"It must have been a ghost." said Philippa, passing me my second cup of coffee.

The idea of ghosts in that sunny morning-room in the prosaic atmosphere of newspapers and eggs and bacon was sufficient to set us all smiling. Even I could be amused and make light of it. I who had suffered so keenly but a short while since.

"I've had trouble with that wardrobe before." Mason remarked. "I've found the doors open and accused the maids of looking inside and not troubling to close them."

"Yes, you have, my dear," Philippa remarked, "and perhaps you'll have the goodness to leave the maids alone in future. They don't like to be falsely accused, and in these days they can afford to be touchy."

"I'll apologise to them singly and severally." Mason said good-humouredly. "I'll go and have a look at that wardrobe after breakfast. Stanley, and see if I can find out what is the matter with it. Yours is the first complaint because you're the first to have slept in that room. You see, you're our first guest."

I told them that I was honoured, and after breakfast Mason and I went up to my room together.

Mason was as full of theories as myself on the effect of weather and temperature on wood, but I could see that the wardrobe baffled him. He strained at each of the brass knobs in turn, but could not force open any of the doors without a direct half-turn of the wrist. He looked at me and laughed.

"Well, I don't understand the damned thing!" he said. "What beats me is how this door here came open with such force as to send the chair spinning. Would you like another room tonight?"

"Oh, that's all right, thanks," I laughed. One can afford to laugh in broad sunlight; and to have accepted his offer would have been an admission of misgivings for which the Masons would never cease to laugh at me.

"Well, I'll get a carpenter to come and look at it," said Mason: and of course he forgot.

It was not until I actually entered my room that night that my misgivings returned. Two of Mason's new neighbours had joined us at dinner, good souls both, and we had laughed intermittently throughout the evening. To-night I was in a state of high good humour when I reached my bedroom, although I quailed a little as I closed my door and the memories of the previous night assailed me.

But to-night, I assured myself, everything would be different. Last night I had not been well. The whole unpleasant experience had begun with that ghastly dream of being strangled. To-night I should sleep soundly and the wardrobe doors might spring open as they chose. And, true to my intention, I was asleep within twenty minutes.

How long I slept I can hardly say, before once more a galloping fear assailed me in some shapeless dream. Once more I felt that ghastly tightness of the throat. An iron ring slowly and steadily increasing its pressure seemed to encircle it. Once more I tried to struggle, once more I felt myself bring carried rapidly away on a flood of terror towards some nameless abyss. I heard my own harsh, throaty scream as, with God knows what effort, I woke myself at last.

I struggled to a sitting posture, while the sweat from my hair and brow half blinded me. I was breathing as if I had just reached the surface of water after too deep a dive. And as I sat, torn between relief from the dream and the horror of having experienced it, I heard noises from the wardrobe which I shall always remember and yet shall never adequately be able to describe.

Inside that wardrobe something was struggling, even as I had just been struggling in my sleep. The sounds were half human, half bestial, and accompanying them was a harsh creaking, as of a wooden structure straining under too much weight. God help me! I thought of a gallows, and my blood ran cold. A dreadful numbness seized me and I could only sit and stare and suffer.

The spell was broken by the sudden leaping open of one of the middle doors. So quickly and violently did it spring round upon its hinges that it might have been flung open from within by the spasmodic lashing out of a man's foot. On the instant I came tumbling out of bed.

I had flung all my pride from me. I did not care what anybody thought or said. I had had more than enough of that room and that wardrobe. I knew I could not endure such another night as the last, and to-night promised to be worse. I must rouse Mason and be must find me another room.

Every ounce of my remaining moral strength I summoned to make myself approach that wardrobe. Just inside the door, which now stood open, my dressing-gown was hanging. I shut my eyes, screwing up the lids, and blundered to it, and groped inside with one hand.

Of the abominable moment which followed, with all its scaring, exquisite terror, the whole indescribable foulness of the experience, I can remember everything. My groping hand encountered something as heavy and solid as a full sack of flour—something heavy and yet soft, which swung under the touch of my fingers, and then rebounded upon them. And on the rebound my hand touched naked flesh, cold and damp and flabby, the hand—how shall I write it?—of a dead man.

Somehow I must have forced my way out of the room, although I remember nothing of it, for Mason heard my cry, and found me a few moments later in a dead faint at the foot of the stairs.

Three months later I had another invitation from the Masons, containing a tactful remark in parenthesis that they would prepare for me a room on the same floor as their own. I accepted the invitation on those conditions, although I could not help but fear that the mere sight of the house would he inexpressibly painful to me. My last visit there had brought me as near to a nervous breakdown as I ever wish to approach.

But we met on the old footing, and none of us alluded to my vile experience on the occasion of my previous visit.

After dinner, however, while we sat around the drawing-room fire, smoking and talking, an instance arose which brought the thing hack again into the light.

I was sitting in a corner nearest to where a great pile of logs lay on the hearth. The fire was burning low and Philippe Mason asked me to replenish it. I threw on a log, and noticed for the first time that the wood was planed on two sides and polished on one.

Mason eyed me curiously.

"Don't you recognise the logs?" he asked.

I shook my head.

"You ought to," he said. "It's your wardrobe."

"You've destroyed it, then?" I asked superfluously.

"Yes", he said, suddenly removing his gaze from me. "We couldn't keep it, and it didn't seem fair to sell it. He looked towards his wife. "Shall we tell him, Philippa?"

I intercepted a shake of the head and meaning frown.

"You found out something about that wardrobe?" I asked quickly.

Neither of them answered. Philippe's dumb show had left Mason penitent and embarrassed.

"Tell me", I urged. "I want to know.

"It might upset you a bit, old man," Mason stammered apologetically.

"No it won't; but if you found out anything about that accursed piece of furniture, for Heaven's sake tell."

Philippa rose and took my glass.

"You'll have a whiskey and soda, won't you, Stanley?" she asked, and shapely removed it to a small table, on which a tantalus stood, at a far end of the long room.

"Well, matter of fact," began Mason a little shakily, "it came about in this. It leaked out locally that I knew a bit about old Bibles, and a fellow named Hanlon wrote me a civil note and asked if he might bring one to show me. He'd picked it up somewhere, and wanted to know if it was worth anything. Of course, I wrote back and told him to bring it along; which he did. I'm afraid he was appointed over his Bible, and I soon set his mind at rest. He'd got hold of an old Coverdale, and there are hundreds of them knocking about. But we gave him tea, and chattered over various things, and then it emerged that he was one of Hanlons who used to live at Chilby Hall.

"'Oh!' said I, 'I've got a great wardrobe upstairs that came from there.' And I told him how it had come into my hands. He asked to see it, and I took him up and showed it to him. When he'd seen it he turned and looked at me with a funny little lift of the eyebrows.

"'You're a brave man,' he said, 'to have that thing inside your house.' As soon as he'd spoken he could see that he'd touched a tender spot and wanted to dry up. But I wouldn't let him and pressed him for more.

"'Oh,' he said, that wardrobe was one of the family superstitions. It was never used in my time. We used to keep it shut up in a big lumber-room. My great grandfather, who was no end of buck, had it made for him. There were all sorts of stories told about him and his clothes in his heyday, before he gambled away everything outside the entail."

"'But,' I asked, 'why was there supposed to be something sinister about that wardrobe?"

"He looked at me and uttered a little uncomfortable laugh.

"'Well, you see,' he said, 'when the old boy had come to the end of everything, he hanged himself inside that wardrobe from one of the beams.'"

At Mrs Questney's

On the instant I felt myself shuddering and my teeth chattering. Since the curtains had been drawn the atmosphere of the room had become oppressively hot, but now a sudden icy wind invaded it, cutting through my clothes and skin like a breath from the Arctic. Then once more came that crack from the table.

There are advantages attached to leading the unfashionable life of the suburbans apart from providing amusement for the very smart. For instance, after a dinner-party one's hosts, and fellow-guests do not break up into shoals and rush off to other houses soon as they have been fed. One is there for a long evening, and one can dance or play bridge or talk with the comfortable assurance that the next move will be for home and bed, and that one's entertainers will not begin to throw covert glances at the clock until after midnight. My simple and bourgeois temperament is adapted to this mode of living, for, once having feasted, I want to feel anchored for the evening.

The Questneys' dinner-parties, given at their home at Wimbledon, have always been entertainments which I should be sorry to have missed. It is no affair of mine if the food were sent down ready cooked by a firm of London caterers. The atmosphere is always homely, in the best sense of the word. There is no attempt at display, and one is waited on by the same two grim and elderly parlour-maids who are always on duty on less formal occasions. Moreover, there have always been at least three others whom I can meet at the bridge table on terms of equality.

Of course, there are freaks even in the Questneys' circle, but they are to be found everywhere. I dare say Messrs. Barnum and Bailey recruited from every nationality and every stratum of society. The mental freak is just as universal. Mayfair women talk about their " mahatmas and aspire to achieving a rigor mortis of the mind which they call Nirvana.

Cornish fishermen with gumboils go to see "white-witches" instead of consulting dentists. Wimbledon would be odd indeed if it did not contain a few oddities.

There is, for example, Mr. Gillett, who would have me to believe that my sturdy British stock sprang from the East, and that my descendants will be the ultimate inheritors of the earth. He prophesies by means of the Pyramids, and, undeterred by the cynical smile of the Sphinx, has given the dates of at least seven tribulations, all safely passed over without any more cataclysmal happening than the defeat of Lancashire in a cricket match. But he goes on prophesying without apology for former inaccuracies, and, by the latest advice, the rising of Antichrist has been postponed until the middle of the March after next.

Mrs. Twill, on the other hand without entirely subscribing to Mr. Gillett's uncomfortable creed, is sympathetic to every belief which is sufficiently groundless. She tells her own fortune by cards every day, and so achieves a brand-new future every twenty-four hours. She has had her horoscope cast by seven different mystics and, according to two of them, she is already dead. She has been to more unsatisfactory seances than any other woman in England, but clings affectionately to the belief that her late uncle, the archdeacon, whacked her over the head with a tambourine, and that her nephew who was killed in the war told her through a trumpet that he was running a retail sweets and tobacco business just outside the realms of light.

Miss Ensell is another. I have not tried to pierce the veils which shroud the abysmal recesses of her mind, but I know that she once marched to Trafalgar Square bearing a banner with the strange device, "Be Kind to Doggie and Pussy" and that she belongs to a league which is sworn to abolish capital punishment.

I mention these three because they were all at the Questneys' on the June evening of which I am about to write. There were a dozen of us, all told, and the remaining nine, including Mr. and Mrs. Questney, were assorted but mainly average people. I knew them all with varying degrees of intimacy, so that I was Mr. Greendale to one half of the dozen and Jack to the other half.

THE dinner was a long one, and we men lingered some while over the table after the ladies were gone, so that it was already dusk when we rejoined them in the drawing-room. I saw, then, that it was going to be a night of talk. Somebody remarked that it was too hot for dancing, and I heard no dissentient voice. Nor did Mrs. Questney look around with the contemplative gaze of one considering the personnel of three well-balanced bridge tables.

So we sat and talked, and, of course, Mrs. Twill, Miss Ensell, and Gillett all mounted their hobby-horses in turn; and, unfortunately, Dick Cordrey was in one of his frivolous moods.

Dick Cordrey is a very good fellow, but I have heard him described at times as—well, you know—not quite, and unable altogether to conceal the hairy hoof. He has no reverence for the beliefs of others when he considers them ridiculous, nor is he any sparer of feelings. Very soon he had the weird three writhing with indignation, and I saw the Questneys begin to fidget uncomfortably.

"What I want to know," he said to Mrs. Twill, "is why your spirits, which seem to be voluble enough and to take the greatest interest in mundane affairs, are never able to vouchsafe any information which is of the least use to any of us."

"But they do," protested Mrs. Twill. "There is one medium—I can tell you her name—whose clients do very well on the Stock Exchange."

"Then they oughtn't merely to do very well; they ought all to be millionaires in a few weeks. Very well, then, let's accept that as a fact. The spirits, then, are able to see into the hidden future, but their information about the past—or such of it as we don't know ourselves—is always highly erroneous."

"Not at all," began Mrs. Twill. "Not at—"

"Oh, excuse me! Why, then, after a murder which has baffled the police, don't you people ascertain from the spirits the name of the murderer? I know they try it every time, but events have always proved that they've received the name and description of a non-existent person, or, at any rate, the wrong person altogether. All you've got to do is to summon the spirit of the victim—"

"Yes," said Mrs. Twill bitterly, "approach a sacred subject in the spirit of vulgar curiosity!"

"Scotland Yard may be vulgarly curious," retorted the rude young man, "but it's a highly necessary institution."

"And, I was going to add, you are bound to get frivolous spirits."

"I shouldn't feel frightfully frivolous if I'd just been murdered," somebody remarked. "I should get through to the nearest medium and tell him who'd done it."

"The victims have been purified by death," Miss Ensell interpolated," and they are not revengeful. Besides, they know all and can see for themselves the wickedness of capital punishment."

"Ah!" exclaimed Mrs. Twill, grateful for an ally.

"Then, if they're purified by death, how is it that they're frivolous?" demanded the tenacious and exasperating Cordrey. "It doesn't seem to square.

"There are certain things which we are not meant to know," said Gillett heavily.

Cordrey swung round on this new antagonist, like a Richard or a Godfrey enjoying himself among the Saracens.

"I quite agree with you," he said. "For instance, we evidently aren't meant to know when to expect catastrophes on a large scale, in spite of the Pyramids. According to you, half the world was going to be destroyed last May, but we're still here."

Gillett glared at him as if he were one of the Beasts in Revelation and subsided. Cordrey stepped over the stricken body, so to say, and returned to Mrs. Twill, in whom there was still life and fight.

"If we're not meant to know who's committed a murder, and if the spirit, of the murdered is at once so frivolous as to give us silly answers and so purified as not to desire justice, why do your friends go on holding stances and trying to find out?"

"I maintain," replied Mrs. Twill stoutly," that it would be possible to discover the identity of the murderer from the spirit of the victim, given the proper conditions."

"The conditions!" said Cordrey. "Oh, yes, I forgot. They're always wrong, aren't they?"

"Not always wrong. But if you knew as much of these things as I do you would appreciate the difficulties of getting them exactly right."

Cordrey sighed. He knew that she had fallen back on her last and impregnable line of defence—the Hindenburg Line of her cult.

"Well, Mrs. Twill," he said," it seems a pity to me that some of your friends haven't discovered who murdered Jenny Short and laid their evidence before the police. They've had a week to do it in now. It's a particularly brutal and horrible murder, and if the spirits have any sense of justice they ought to see that the man who did it doesn't get away with it. The police are completely baffled."

I must here digress to refresh certain memories concerning the case of Jenny Short. She was a London typist who had gone to Brighton for her annual holiday. On the tenth night she did not return to her lodgings, and in the morning her murdered body was found on the downs under Ditchling Beacon. She was known to have "gentlemen friends," but her discretion, and theirs, had left the police entirely ignorant of their identities. A hundred false clues had already been sifted and found worthless.

"The murderer will be discovered," said Mrs. Twill, impressively, "and justice will be done. No doubt the spirit of the poor murdered girl knows that quite well and sees no need to make revelations."

"That's all very well," Cordrey protested, "but what guarantee have we of that? There are murderers who escape, you know. Now, Mrs. Twill, you understand this table-turning business, why shouldn't we—here and now, with Mrs. Questney's permission—hold a seance and try to find out who killed Jenny Short?"

"It would be quite useless with you here, Mr. Cordrey" replied Mrs. Twill, with an air of gloomy triumph.

"But why? Please don't think, because I have been arguing, that I am not open to conviction. I promise to approach the subject seriously and reverently. The spirits have no objection to an honest inquirer, surely? But, of course, if you won't accept the challenge—"

Strangely enough, nearly everybody in the room was anxious that Mrs. Twill should accept the challenge. Most of us had played at table-turning before, and had achieved the usual unsatisfactory but inexplicable results. Something which is yet to be scientifically accounted for does set a table in motion and cause it, by rocking's or rapping's, to spell out words and sentences. Unfortunately, it generally spells out gross inaccuracies or incoherent gibberish, and that, Mrs. Twill alleges, is when the mischievous and frivolous spirits are about.

The Questneys' looked doubtful at first, but they gave way. Mrs. Twill, as the acknowledged expert, took charge of the proceedings, "although," she modestly asserted," I have no personal gifts of this kind, and I may as well say in advance that I don't expect any satisfactory results."

She looked about her.

"We shall want a table that we can all get round," she said. "I think that large card-table might be big enough, if we may have it, Mrs. Questney. We mustn't mind being a little crowded. And then we must have all the lights extinguished."

The card-table, one built for round games and not merely for whist or bridge, was opened, and the men drew chairs around it. It was a tight squeeze, but there was just room for the round dozen of us. Mrs. Twill showed us how to rest our finger-tips lightly-on the table, the little fingers of each of us touching those of his neighbours so that a complete chain was formed. Then she said that we must all keep silent and be very serious, thinking only of what we hoped might happen. After which she rose, switched off the lights, and came back to the table.

It was a dark night outside, but sufficient light filtered in through the open windows to enable us to see each other. Mrs. Twill rose again, drew the curtains one by one, and eventually left us in a Stygian gloom which grew more stuffy, moment by moment.

Even to the most irreclaimable Sadducee there is something eerie and impressive in sitting with others in the dark, waiting for a message from the dead, however sure he may be that no such message will come. Speaking for myself, I own that I played the game. It is absurd to scoff at Mrs. Twill and the kind when one has not obeyed the rules. Mundane thoughts invaded my head, but I conscientiously cast them forth. To what extent the others did as they were required I am unable to say.

For a few minutes only the sound of our collective breathing, a few smothered coughs and a faint creaking of chairs broke the silence inside the room. The voices of the outside world invaded without disturbing us. Occasionally cars hummed by along the road outside, and we heard voices and, once, the sound of a boy singing. Somewhere in the room a clock became voluble, and loudly and niggardly released the seconds one by one.

Then Mrs. Twill began to speak in the low, reverent voice of a high-priestess beginning an incantation. She asked from time to time if there were spirits present. If there were, she begged that the spirit of Jenny Short should be summoned. We waited for a long time in vain, and then suddenly, I for one, jumped; for a little explosive crack sounded from somewhere in the middle of the table.

"Is that a spirit present? Mrs. Twill inquired.

Again we heard that crack, meaning Yes.

"Is it the spirit of Jenny Short?" Crack!

The breathing all around me grew louder. Mrs. Twill's voice became self-consciously steadier than ever, as if to show us how little surprised she was, and that this result, so far as it went, was a mere nothing.

"My dear," she said softly. "We are all very sorry for you, and we want to find out, in the cause of human justice, the name of the man who killed your poor body. Will you spell it out for us?" Crack!

I was conscious of a vague excitement which, allied with the stuffiness of the room, turned me giddy for the moment. Mrs. Twill slowly recited the alphabet until she came to G, when the table cracked again. She had to go further next time, and had reached the letter R before the expected interruption came. Then, slowly and ruthlessly, my name was spelt out. "Greendale!" cried half of us at once, and there was general laughter. Even Mrs. Twill herself did not remain altogether grave.

"Ladies and gentlemen," I exclaimed pathetically, "please believe that I didn't do it! I can prove an alibi—twenty alibis. I was at the Savoy Theatre on the night that poor girl was murdered."

I knew who had spelt out my name, although I couldn't think how he had managed to do it, and I felt a qualm of resentment against Cordrey. It wasn't playing the game, especially after his promise.

"It's just as I feared," said Mrs. Twill with a sigh. "We've got some frivolous spirit mocking our efforts. Still, we will try again, if you like. Is Jenny Short there?"

On the instant I felt myself shuddering and my teeth chattering. Since the curtains had been drawn the atmosphere of the room had become oppressively hot, but now a sudden icy wind invaded it, cutting through my clothes and skin like a breath from the Arctic. Then once more came that crack from the table.

"My dear, please don't jest with us, pleaded poor Mrs. Twill. "We want to help justice. Won't you tell us who killed your poor body."

And then, for the second time that evening, my name was spelt out. Mrs. Twill rose and turned on the lights and we all blinked at one another.

"You see," she said," it's quite hopeless. The conditions are not good. We have the wrong spirits here."

I don't know if she suspected Cordrey, but if she did she was too polite to say so, bearing in mind the promise he had given. The curtains were drawn back from the windows, and then, at the invitation of Mrs. Questney, which sounded more like begging than asking, Nell Foster went to the piano and played and sang to us. We had done with mysticism for that night.

Cordrey and I lived near each other so, later, we walked home together. I turned upon him as soon as we were outside the house.

"Thanks," I said, "for spelling out my name."

"Not at all," he answered blandly, "you didn't mind, did you?"

"For myself, not in the least. I knew it was you. Only I don't think it was playing the game to guy the show, especially after you'd promised not to."

He stopped for a moment to light a cigarette.

"No," he agreed, "I see what you mean, but I swear I didn't intend to do it. There was such a crowd of us that I could only get one hand on the table, although none of the others noticed. And suddenly I got an overmastering impulse. I didn't know what an overmastering impulse was before to-night, but I do now. I swear, Jack, that I simply couldn't help myself."

"H'm," I said, "well, having had an overmastering impulse to break your word once, was there any necessity to do it a second time?"

"When?"

"The second time when you spelt out my name."

He laughed shortly.

"But that wasn't me!"

"Who was it then?"

"Nell Foster, I expect. Didn't you notice that the taps came from a different part of the table? I saw a twinkle in her eye before we started. I say, did you notice that beastly cold wind that came into the room?"

"I did," I said shortly. "What was it? Some mechanical phenomenon of yours which you had an overmastering impulse to produce, so as to annoy poor Mrs. Twill?"

He laughed again.

"Not guilty," he said, "It was most impressive, wasn't it? The curtains were drawn over the open windows and we were getting stuffier and stuffier, and I suppose the breeze outside freshened, parted the curtains a little and poured in on us like a cold douche."

"That may have been it" I agreed, "but it's a warm night, and that seemed icy cold to me."

I overslept on the following morning and had to rush to the station, catch my train to the City by the skin of my teeth, and travel to Mark Lane without a paper. My colleague Bromley greeted me as I entered the office.

"Hello, Murderer," he said. "Thought they'd got you safely quodded."

I recognised the allusion and stared at him in amazement, wondering whom he was likely to know that had been a guest of the Questneys, on the preceding evening. But I answered stiffly:

"I don't follow."

"Don't you read the papers?" he asked, grinning.

"No time this morning," I explained, shortly.

"Oh, then, you don't know. The police have arrested a man in connection with that murder on the Downs. Of course, I was only joking, and he's no relation of yours, old man. But his name's Greendale all right."

The House by the Crossroads

This is a story of sixty years ago, and a story almost forgotten even in Murlinhurst, although some of the greyheads, recalling the days of their childhood, speak of strange things that happened in the House by the Crossroads, and still glance at it with a reminiscent interest as they pass it by.

The old house is empty now save for an elderly couple who keep the rooms aired and are ever in readiness to act as guides to the prospective tenant who never comes. They have no nerves, these two, and would live cheerfully with the devil had his house a roof to cover them. The village people will have nothing to do with them, and they never talk of the things that happen in the old house—except to me.

Three days ago I was passing, and the whim took me to call and see them. It was a bright, warm day, with a fresh breeze blowing, and the cherry blossom from the trees above was falling in showers at the foot of the wall. A Kentish village, when the cherry blossom is out, is a sight that hurts one who has seen the same pageant for eighty successive years and knows well that an unseen hand will beckon before another spring comes round. There were wallflowers blooming in the deserted garden, and the scent of them came to me like a tune out of the past; for a scent recalls a memory sooner than a song or a face or a scene, and the old war-horse, smelling powder, will snort and try to plunge with his stiff old legs.

Smelling the wallflowers, I turned as if a voice had called me, and pushed open the heavy iron gate. It creaked to a dreary tune as I forced it back on its hinges, the same complaining squeal, I thought, as it was wont to give sixty years ago. I walked up the weed-grown drive with the Past keeping pace beside me, and for the moment I was young again, and half expected to see old Martha come out and shake a mat, or Beatrice smile at me from one of the uncurtained windows.

I rang the bell, and Wicks the caretaker came to the door and touched a white forelock at the sight of me. We are good friends, Wicks and I, for I bring him tobacco, and he knows the story of my connection with the sad old house. 'You look sleepy,' I said to him presently, seeing that he had some ado to keep his bloodshot eyes open.

He nodded.

'Oh, ay, 'twas a moonlight night last night, and they kept us both awake. Lord Francis he rode up on his horse and made a deal of clatter outside the house, and Miss Beatrice she was screaming half the night and rushing from room to room, and aft'wards we could hear the scuffle and thud in the library as plain as plain. We're not afeard, the missus and me, but it don't give us much chance to sleep. '

He spoke quite calmly there in the sunlight with the flowers and long weeds in the garden whisking and turning in the morning breeze. He could not have spoken more evenly and naturally of living people, and yet those who had disturbed his rest had been dead for sixty years. Indeed, I think he had come to regard them almost as living people.

'They are a long time finding rest,' I said sadly.

'Oh, ay, a long time,' he agreed. 'As I've a-told Mr Dickson, he might just as well pull down the house, for no one won't ever live in it 'cept the missus and me.'

I thought so, too, although the rent is reduced to almost a tenth of what it used to be; and doubtless in time Mr Dickson will come to the same conclusion and the housebreakers will level it to the ground. But I am glad that it will not be in my day. The old House by the Crossroads is a temple of memories, merry and pleasant as well as sad and terrible.

As I turned away I thought that I would set myself at once to the task of writing out the story of the house and the people who lived in it in the days when our King's grandmother was yet a young woman.

I had meant to for years, but now in the nature of things my days cannot be long, and there is danger in procrastinating when one is turned eighty. So here is the story of Beatrice and the three men who loved her, and the tragedy brought about by the love of those two who would not stand aside.

In those days the old House by the Crossroads was occupied by two middle-aged gentlewomen, the Misses Mainsley, and their niece, Beatrice Trenion. Beatrice, the daughter of their married sister, left an orphan at the age of two, had been adopted by the two ladies, who took the child in from a sense of duty and ended by loving her as if she were their own daughter. There was something strangely pathetic in the way those two plain, angular maiden ladies mothered and watched over little Beatrice, and, in accordance with the custom of the day, carefully withheld from her such little knowledge of life as they themselves possessed.

They were poor for those autocratic days when most gentlefolk seemed to have money, and the House by the Crossroads was not a large one. I know that callers made it a rule not to take the two gentle old creatures by surprise, for then one saw that they were not comfortable, and presently old Martha, the house-parlourmaid, might be observed running out to the village shop to buy cake. Miss Mary, the elder, wrote verses, which were generally acclaimed in the neighbourhood as being quite as good as those of the lady who won fame as 'L.E.L.', and Miss Jane had a gift for stitching samplers; but they spent most of the time in which they were not engaged upon the lighter housework in making undergarments for the poor and visiting the sick of the parish. Two good, simple ladies they were, of a breed long since died out.

My father was the local doctor, and his practice among the poor brought him into frequent contact with the Misses Mainsley, so that by the time I was a stripling we were almost like one family, with the vicarage people as cousins. My father was a widower, and to this day I am certain that he loved Miss Mary and that she would have married him but for strong virginal prejudices. I—well, of course, I fell in love with Beatrice.

She was a pretty little thing as I remember her first, with dark hair and eyes, and—what was not admired in those days—a determined little chin.

Every Sunday I used to go to the old House by the Crossroads to tea, and after tea Miss Mary and Miss Jane would give Beatrice and me religious instruction. Before tea, however, when I strongly suspect the two elder ladies took a siesta, Beatrice and I had the run of the house and garden to ourselves. We were supposed to read and discuss certain books given to us by the aunts, and the memory of those dear old priggish stories brings a smile to my lips and a lump in my throat. 'Willie's Christmas Dinner, or Who Told the Curate?' 'Bessie's Downfall' (which, in spite of its title, was quite fit for children, concerning as it did the theft of a rice pudding and the subsequent mental torture of the little thief), 'Uncle Jim's Sunday Afternoon Chats with Little Christians'—dear, dear! I remember them all.

I was twelve and Beatrice ten when I first proposed to her. About that time we could trust each other well enough to admit in hushed voices that Willie and Bessie and Uncle Jim palled after a time. We therefore neglected them on the Sabbath afternoons, and since we were not allowed to play hide and seek we played at love.

Beatrice rejected me at first for a whole month because I refused to follow the custom of the day and propose on my knees. After a while, however, she climbed down, as I knew she would. Even then I was only allowed to kiss her once in a while. Beatrice did not consider it proper.

Dear old days they were, and the knowledge that we had a secret which must be kept at all costs from the aunts added a zest to life. I remember once that they surprised us in the midst of a quarrel, and try as they would, could not get to the root of the trouble, which was simply that I had refused to pretend that Beatrice's most repulsive-looking doll was our eldest daughter. As I grew up I found that the game of love had become a real thing to me, and Beatrice imagined for the time that the old sisterly affection was something stronger. The aunts never knew, but old Martha one day surprised us and kept our secret like the good woman she was. In memory of that and of other kindnesses I see that her gravestone is kept as white as any in the village churchyard.

As we grew older, Martha it was who risked her place by passing notes between us; and it was at her connivance that I spent three long hours one night alone in the garden with Beatrice. That night, with the moonlight flooding the well-ordered garden, and the child-like face beside me with its strangely-shining eyes, is my pleasantest and most vivid memory; and I think that on the day I get to Heaven—if I ever do—I shall fancy that I have been there before, seeing a moonlit garden and a face out of my childhood close to me.

Good old days, and poor old Martha! I know she used to pray for us—I know she used to shed tears over the thought of the two young lovers. It was her one ambition to see us wedded, and she would have willingly laid down her simple old life to bring about that consummation. I was eighteen when she warned me that I had a rival. Beatrice was sixteen then, and regarded as husband-high.

'Master Ned,' she whispered to me one evening, meeting me alone in the village street, 'far be it from me to urge you on to do anything rash, but if I was a young man as wanted to marry a certain young lady I should take it and do it at once; run off with her I should!'

'What do you mean?' I asked quickly.

'And if so be as you've not started to make money as yet, Martha Smith has got a stocking with near a hundred pounds in it. '

I thanked her as best I could, but declined her well-meant offer. Young and inexperienced as I was I knew that a hundred pounds was not enough to begin married life on. Besides, Beatrice would never run away with me. She was much too gentle and dutiful in spite of her determined little chin. 'I'll wait,' I said, 'until I've money of our own, and then I can go to Aunt Jane and -'

'My dear, blessed boy,' Martha interrupted, 'you don't surely think that the old ladies mean Miss Beatrice for the likes of you—beggin' your pardon for putting it that way. They tell me things, you know, which I'm expected not to repeat. They want her to marry Lord Francis Brentford.'

The news was like a blow across the face to me. Lord Francis was a son of the Marquis of Stoneharden, a distant connection of the aunts. I had met him at their house two or three times, and had wondered why he troubled to visit two very uninteresting old ladies, but passed the matter over in my mind with the reflection that blood was thicker than water.

He had always struck me as a tremendously grand personage with modish ways and beautiful clothes and a way of addressing women that made me feel like a young barbarian beside him. He had also beautiful side-whiskers which I envied from the bottom of my heart. But until then I had neither liked nor disliked him, feeling quite content that he took but little notice of me. Both the aunts were loud in his praises, declaring him to be very genteel, and flattering him to his face by calling him a quizz. Those were the days when everybody was reading Jane Eyre, and despairing of ever attaining to Lord Francis's courtliness I had determined to model myself upon the blunt, super-masculine Mr Rochester.

'How do you know that, Martha?' I asked quickly.

'Do you think I don't know most things what go on in their minds, let alone what they tell me?' old Martha retorted, 'I've been a servant in the family nigh thirty years, and I ain't quite strangers with them. Why, I knew Miss Mary and Miss Jane when they were almost lasses. I tell you this, Master Ned, Lord Francis has taken a fancy to Miss Beatrice and said as much to the mistresses, and they're main pleased to hear it.'

She saw me wince, and smiled at me out of her faded blue eyes, if you'll listen to me,' she said again, 'you'll take and run off with Miss Beatrice, and God forgive me for saying it.'

I knew nothing against Lord Francis then. He was not from our part of the country, and it was not until I heard my father speak of him that I knew something of his character. Even then I knew that he was no worse than a thousand others, but that side of him gave me something definite to take hold of and hate. It was not nice to think of Beatrice mated with that animal.

When I spoke to her of him a few days later I was relieved to find that she did not like him. Afterwards, when the aunts began to hint to her and she began to understand, she hate him much more than it was considered ladylike to hate anyone, and I think she loved me better than she had ever done before or did since. The aunts did not press her at first, and Lord Francis was in no hurry to marry, so time flowed smoothly on until two more years were spent.

Then, one evening, I called and found Beatrice in tears.

Aunt Mary had spoken sharply to her, blamed her for her obstinacy, and commanded her to accept her kinsman. Duty—Christian duty—was a word she used time and again during the homily. Was it for this that they had brought her up and lavished money upon her education and training? As for love—it was improper of a young girl to think of loving a man before she married him!

They had reduced her to tears, but not to quiescence. They had counted without that determined little chin. As for me—I do not think they ever fancied Beatrice could ever love me except as a brother, and in that at least events proved them to be right. But Beatrice thought then that she cared for me, and on that night of nights she rested a long while in my arms with her wet face touching mine.

'Beatrice,' I said in my great gruff 'Rochester' voice, 'promise you won't give in—promise me you'll never marry that man.'

'I never will, Ned,' she answered firmly.

And then I thought that nothing could come between us.

It was less than a fortnight afterwards that my father took a resident patient, a young man named Stephen Burgess, who had been gazetted only a few months since. He had been badly taken with scarlet fever and needed the country air, but I think his parents were anxious to keep him away from his regiment for a while and made the most of their opportunity.

He was a merry, rackety fellow who had certainly gone the pace, and on the first night he came to us, as we sat up smoking our churchwardens in the parlour after my father had gone to bed, I found myself regarding him with that mingled awe and admiration which I had once felt for Lord Francis Brentford.

He told me tales of desperate escapades at Sandhurst, and we both laughed over his stories until the house rang with our merriment, and my father called downstairs and threatened to order his patient to bed. Then we spoke of the expected war with Russia, and Stephen was very anxious to see some fighting. He had the situation at his finger tips, and explained to me, with the aid of rough drawings, how the Crimean peninsula would be the seat of war if France and Britain went to Turkey's aid.

From war we switched the conversation off on to love, and Stephen told me tales of his own conquests that took my breath away. He was undeniably a braggart, but there was a certain freshness about him that robbed his egotism of any offence. He confessed himself to be in love with at least a dozen girls, but disclaimed any intention to marry. 'My dear fellow, what is the use of a wife to a fighting man?'

When he paused I was moved to tell him in strict confidence of my love affair with Beatrice. I had never told anyone before, and it was strange that I should have been moved to tell this boisterous, joke-cracking fellow on the first night of our acquaintance. When I told him all, he looked at me with a new kind of respect that was almost comic.

'And you've loved each other ever since you were children?' he exclaimed.

I told him that such was the case.

'And never thought of any other girl?'

'Never!'

'Crikey!' he gasped, and sat silent for a moment as if trying to reckon up how many times he had lost his heart.

'I say,' he said presently, 'why don't you bolt with her?'

I shook my head resolutely. I had the future to consider besides my father and the aunts.

'Well,' said he, 'you're a bulldog for hanging on, and I'd like to help you. We must make this Lord Francis fellow see he isn't wanted. I say, I hope you'll soon give me the opportunity of meeting your inamorata.'

I promised that I would, and then I think we went to bed.

On the following day the aunts bade me to tea, and I obtained an invitation for Stephen and brought him with me.

That afternoon has ever been fresh in my memory from the time we started out together to when we walked home side by side in silence, I with a new pain at my heart which I hardly understood.

The Misses Mainsley received us in the drawing-room, looking as stiff and prim as their solid furniture. I can see them now, bending over their knitting and keeping up a steady flow of polite but exhausting conversation. I remember Stephen provoking the shadow of a frown by allowing his antimacassar to slip down so that the back of his head touched the leather upholstery of the chair, and the comical half-wink he gave me after the word of mild reproof from Miss Mary. We spent some twenty minutes discussing the probable ending of the latest Dickens novel, then appearing in monthly parts, and a little book of poems by Alfred Tennyson, who had already achieved recognition. Stephen was restless and bored, caring little for literature except Bell's Life. Then, just as the ormolu clock tinkled out the hour of four behind its glass case, came a tap at the door, and Beatrice entered the room.

Stephen got smartly on his legs and stood stiff like one on parade, awaiting the necessary words of introduction. As Aunt Mary pronounced them I watched Beatrice closely and with a faint stirring of dismay.

The colour had come suddenly into her face and her gaze was directed in a fixed stare upon Stephen. But for her confusion, which was obvious to us all, she would have looked like one suddenly mesmerised. I transferred my gaze to Stephen, who stood with his lips just parted, staring back at her. There was no recognition in the look he gave her—only a sort of rapt intentness. I was aware of the clock ticking solemnly through the silence like a warning voice, and of frowns settling themselves upon the smooth brows of the aunts.

'Beatrice!' said Aunt Jane sharply, in a tone of horrified amazement.

She started ever so lightly and made the curtsy which young girls were then taught in the schoolroom, and I heard Stephen's chair creak as he settled down into it once more. Beatrice came over to me and gave me her hand. It lay in my own for a moment as cold as ice, and I could feel the little pulse fluttering like a caged bird.

She sat beside me, and I said something light to relieve the silence that seemed to have settled over the room, but Heaven knows my heart was heavy. For I felt that just as Beatrice had gazed upon Stephen at that their first meeting, so had another Beatrice gazed at Dante in the streets of Venice five hundred years before.

'Beatrice, my dear child,' said Aunt Jane, 'I fear that you are indisposed.'

'It is of no importance, thank you, Auntie,' Beatrice rejoined. 'I have only a slight headache.'

I saw the aunts looked relieved. Headaches were then very fashionable and genteel. No nice young girl was really complete without one. Glancing across at Stephen I could guess that he was praying for something to relieve a situation that threatened to become intolerable, for no one seemed to have another word to say, and each tick of the clock was a torment to our jangled nerves. Then a diversion came from an unexpected source. Martha tapped, entered, and announced Lord Francis Brentford.

A minute later he was in the room and bowing over the fingers of the two elder ladies. There was something of the proprietor in his manner as he afterwards saluted Beatrice, and something delightfully off-handed in the way he bowed to me. Immediately afterwards Aunt Mary ceremoniously made him acquainted with Stephen, who, I could see, had taken an instant dislike to him.

He treated Stephen, as he had always treated me, with his well-bred air of indifference, but Stephen met him on his own ground

'Aw! Are you in the Army?' he drawled.

Lord Francis made a negative gesture.

'No, I have not the pleasure,' he answered.

'Aw! I thought not,' Stephen murmured, passing a hand through his long hair. 'Well, you're going to miss something, begad! We and the Turkeys and Froggies are going to meet the Russians soon, and I wouldn't be left out of it for a king's ransom.'

'War,' said Aunt Mary very sharply, 'is a horrible thing!'

What she really meant to say was, how dared Stephen try to make himself a more picturesque character than Lord Francis in the presence of Beatrice.

'My brother,' said his lordship, regarding the tips of his elegant boots, 'is a major in the-th.'

'They ran away in the Afghan campaign,' Stephen observed, 'but doubtless they have acquired some courage since.'

Lord Francis looked pointedly away from him.

'It is the privilege of young men who have never smelt powder,' he said, 'to criticise the conduct of those who have.'

I saw the aunts looking very displeased, and silently begged Stephen with a quick frown not to continue the discussion. It was a relief to us all when we went into the dining-room for tea.

Lord Francis was placed next to Beatrice, and I saw him proffer her very delicate attention, but she answered him only in monosyllables, and her gaze was ever straying across the table and encountering that of Stephen. Jealousy sharpened my sight, and I noticed that every time their gaze met a flush crept into her cheeks. I do not think they exchanged half a dozen words, but there was something written on both their faces that I could not help but read.

Before Stephen and I took our departure, Aunt Jane called me on one side.

'Ned,' she said, 'I do not like your friend. It is intolerable that a kinsman of ours should be insulted in this house by a stranger. I shall be obliged if you do not bring him here again.'

I was madly jealous, but I tried hard to be a sportsman.

'I don't think Burgess meant any harm,' I said. 'He is a nice fellow when you know him.'

'We do not want to know him,' Miss Jane retorted. 'My sister and I both find his breeding intolerable.'

There was nothing more to be said after that, and presently Stephen and I found ourselves walking down the drive together. A feeling of dull depression had settled upon me. I had nothing of which to accuse Stephen, and since I felt that I could not attack him straightforwardly as was my wont, I was awkward and aloof now that we were alone together. In those days I was very much upon my dignity, and I would not for the world have let him see that I was aware of the impression which he had so obviously made upon Beatrice. The young lover, finding himself in the way of being supplanted by a rival, tries to pretend to the world in general that he has noticed nothing. Stephen, too, seemed to be ill at ease, and presently, so oppressive was the silence between us, I asked him what he thought of Lord Francis. 'I shall tell him dooced quick when I get the chance,' Stephen growled.

'Rabbit-faced, cane-sucking idiot!

'The aunts are very fond of him,' I muttered.

'They would be,' he answered, with a twist of contempt distorting his handsome mouth.

'And Beatrice?' I said suddenly, forcing the words from my lips. 'What do you think of her?'

He did not answer, nor did we look at each other.

During the next few succeeding days I saw nothing of Beatrice. I did not meet her out, nor did I call, for I was afraid to discover changes in her towards myself. It seemed ridiculous to imagine that she should have any strong regard for Stephen at that their first meeting, and I strove to reason with myself. But the more I endeavoured to dissuade myself, the more I knew intuitively that my fears were well founded.

I tried to make Stephen say something that would set my mind at rest, but directly I touched upon the subject of love he deftly turned the course of the conversation. I marked certain definite changes in him. He was much more subdued, and far less inclined to boast. Once I tried to get him to speak of his myriad love affairs, and he seemed almost inclined to take offence at being reminded of them.

'Rubbish!' he cried. 'That wasn't love! It was only fun—and besides I was quite a boy. I never really cared for any one of them.'

I do not think that he grew to dislike me, indeed, I am sure he did not, but at that time he often showed a disinclination for my companionship, and wandered about by himself, often coming in late to meals to the expressed annoyance of my father.

At length my continued absence from the House by the Crossroads became noticeable, and I received a note from Miss Mary Mainsley, bidding me to tea. There was nothing for it but to go as an alternative to giving offence, and as I set out I knew that I should return with all uncertainties swept away—either with a new lease of happiness or a burden of despair that I dared hardly think of.

The aunts were engaged when I arrived, and old Martha told me to go out into the garden to Beatrice. I found her on the lawn cutting roses, her hands encased in gardener's gloves. As I crossed the lawn towards her I did not care to look her in the face, and I was thankful that she dropped her scissors so that I might pick them up.

Then 'Ned,' she said; and touched me on the arm.

I looked her straight in the eyes when she spoke to me, and thus it was some time before the scissors found their way from my hand to hers.

'You've quite deserted us,' she said, trying to smile.

'I've been busy,' I muttered.

'Still, you needn't avoid old friends who live only a stone's-throw away from you. It was I who made Aunt Mary write to you this afternoon. I want to talk to you, Ned.'

I said nothing, and stood waiting to hear what she had to say, wondering if she could hear the heavy thumping of my heart. She was silent for a moment, and then:

'Shall we go into the summer house?' she said.

So we went there together, I looking down and grinding my heels upon the daisies as I walked. It was in the wooden summer house, now long since rotted away, that our earliest confidences had been exchanged after the Sunday books had been set aside. It seemed almost as if life as I counted it had begun there, and that there it must end. I knew already the gist of what I was going to hear, and waited dully to listen to the details and to Beatrice's tearful words of regret.

We sat there side by side like the children of eight years before, and I felt like the boy of those days, shy once more, and full of a child's sullen passion and closer to tears than I would have cared to admit.

'Well?' I said presently.

She caught both my hands and burst out crying.

'Ned,' she sobbed, 'dear old Ned, how can I tell you?'

And for the first time in her life she raised her head and kissed me unasked upon the lips.

'Beatrice,' I cried, 'you needn't tell me. I know! You don't love me anymore. '

'Yes, yes I do!' she cried quickly. 'Oh, Ned, you know I do. How can I help loving you after all these years? But—but I think I have only loved you as I might have loved a brother. There is a different kind of love, and I did not know until now. '

'It—it's Stephen Burgess,' I said hoarsely, and I felt her hands tighten on mine.

After all these years an echo of the pain comes back. There are compensations in old age, for Time brings with it a subtle drug, and I know that I could not suffer now as I suffered then.

She was the only creature I had ever loved save my father, and love between men is a thing almost devoid of softness. My mother had died before I was old enough to remember her. And sitting beside Beatrice in the summer house I suddenly found myself alone in the world without love, lonelier than Robinson Crusoe on his island. It is horrible to write, but I think I should have been less unhappy had Beatrice died. Then, suddenly, floodgates in my head and heart were burst asunder, and I found myself begging and imploring her to unsay the terrible words. I am sixty years distant from the shame of that afternoon, and now I may write what I would have no one know—that the water kept coming to my eyes, and that I could not always blink it back.

It was absurd, I argued in my stubborn passion. How could she love a man she had scarcely seen, a man, who, for all she knew, might be the greatest scoundrel on earth. How could she prefer him to me, who had always loved her and faithfully served her. I upbraided her, too, and heaped reproach after reproach upon her little bowed head, and the memory of those reproaches often comes between me and sleep.

She listened to me patiently and in silence until I could say no more.

'It's no use saying I'm sorry,' she murmured. 'You don't believe it, do you, Ned?'

'I don't care whether you're sorry or not,' I answered rudely. 'You've played fast and loose with me, and now you discard me like an old glove after all these years at the sight of a fresh face.'

'I did not know what love was,' was all she could answer.

'But you've only seen him once,' I cried.

She shook her head.

'No, no,' she stammered. "We've met since. We've been meeting every day. But the first time I saw Stephen, I knew!'

I did not understand; indeed, I have never understood. But I suppose there are people whom Nature made the complement of one another and who must know each other when they meet. Beatrice tried to explain, but with a diffident reserve as if anxious to spare me as much pain as possible 'Ned,' she whispered, 'have you ever dreamed something and known nothing about it when you woke in the morning, but remembered it during the day at some sight or sound? When I saw Stephen for the first time I knew that I had always loved him. I can't explain. I am only eighteen years old, but my memory seemed to go back for centuries and lose itself in a mist in which only his face was clear. I knew him! I must have known him in a crowded street. He came into dreams I had long before my soul came to earth. But you don't understand, Ned; you can't understand!'

She was right. I was only twenty; how could I understand? Since then I have heard people talk laughingly or seriously of affinities, and at least I have learned the dictionary meaning of the word.

'Ned,' she went on, 'I'm miserable because of you. You're not angry? Say you forgive me. You wouldn't like me to be unhappy, Ned?'

I was not angry with her and forgave her very rapidly. My grudge was all against Stephen, who had stolen her away from me, for in those days a young man considered a girl as a creature entirely passive. I think she wanted me to kiss her, but I did not do so. There was a shadow between us, the shadow of Stephen, and my knuckles were itching to jar against his teeth.

She seemed to guess that an almost murderous hatred was raging in my head, for presently she said, 'And you mustn't blame Stephen, either. It was no more his fault than mine.'

'No,' I burst out, 'I suppose I must sit still and let myself be supplanted by whomsoever takes the trouble. I must be the gentle, patient man like the fools in those books we used to read on Sunday. Bah! the creatures in them had milk instead of blood in their veins. While I'm a man with a man's muscles I'll play the man's game. If we lived fifty years ago I would have called him out and shot him.'

'No, you would not,' she said in her gentle, wheedling voice. 'You wouldn't like me to be miserable always, would you, Ned? I should like to love you best for the sake of the old days which are ended now. But it isn't our fault. It was none of us who had the writing of the book of Fate. Stephen feels as I do. He understood directly we met that afternoon in the drawing-room.'

'Of course he said so,' I sneered.

I would have loved then to tell her of the dozens of love affairs of which Stephen had boasted to me, but I had a sense of honour which, I thank Heaven, has always prevented me from sinking below a certain depth. Even then I made up my mind that I would hit above the belt. Stephen and I would settle our quarrel like men.

Beatrice got upon her feet and I did likewise. I felt sick and giddy and swayed as I stood. She saw, and her hand was on my arm.

'Ned!' she said.

I must have loved her rather finely, as perhaps only a boy can love, for I managed to smile in an attempt to reassure her.

'I'm all right, Beatrice,' I said, 'don't worry about me. Only—only things are all mixed up and upside down. Life's got into a terrible tangle this last few days. I—I want to think things out—that's all!'

She gave a little pull at my sleeve. I could see how relieved she was that the brief interview was over.

'Let's go in to tea,' she said.

I shook my head resolutely. 'Tea! No, Beatrice, I must go.'

Her face fell.

'Oh,' she cried, 'but what shall I tell the aunts? They will think it so strange.'

'Say I'm not well—anything. How could I sit still and talk to them now, when—Oh, Beatrice, you understand!'

She understood quite well and did not argue further, but let me out by a side gate near the stables, and once free of her presence I set off down the road at five miles an hour, more mad than sane. At home, the maid who let me in told me that my father had gone off to visit a patient, but that Mr Burgess was in the garden. I took off my coat in the hall and went out to him. All the bad blood in my body had gone to my head, and I looked forward to smashing his face with a pleasure almost voluptuous. He was lounging on a seat when I set foot on the gravel path.

'You're soon back,' he remarked, looking up; and then he saw my face, and his own changed colour.

'Yes, I am,' I cried, 'and I've come to look for you, you cur.'

He got quickly upon his legs. He had no need to ask me to explain myself. Words were not needed nor wasted on either side just then. I checked myself for a moment to give him time to take off his coat, but he seemed to prefer not to. Those were the days when young men fought like dogs over a quarrel instead of sulking and sneering like wenches.

We were well matched in size, myself shorter, but a little   stouter and larger of limb than he. He squared up to me in a fine bustling style, but I went crashing through his guard and down he went with his cheek-bone laid bare and blood streaming over his face and neck. I drew back, thinking the fight was over and done with, but he was up again like an india-rubber ball, and before I knew it he was at my throat, and we went down together, I on my back and he sprawling across my body.

He had my throat between the thumb and first finger of each hand, and the torment of my crushed windpipe and strangled breath sapped all the strength out of my body. I smashed at his face with both fists for a moment, but he clung like a bull terrier, and then a dreadful weakness seized upon me. My tongue came out and lolled from side to side of my mouth. A great black cloud seemed to gather in the sky, and then descend and blot out everything.

When I came to, he was fanning me with a book. His face was tenderly white save where it was dark with bruises and red with the blood that still streamed from it.

'My God!' he breathed. 'I thought I had killed you.'

I sat up weak and shaken.

'You don't fight fair!' I cried.

'I know,' he muttered. 'I—I've got a murderous temper I let go just in time. You never gave me a chance to speak to you, Ned. God knows I've wronged you, just as He knows it's no fault of mine or hers. I wanted to tell you about it before, but she would not let me. She wanted to tell you herself. Did she tell you how sorry I -'

'Damn it,' I gasped, touching my sore throat with the tips of my fingers,

'I don't want your pity! You don't fight fair, you coward.'

'I know,' he answered, humbly, 'and I never fight. I wouldn't have fought with you, but you gave me no chance to do anything else. I think I'd sooner have run away, Ned.'

Such talk sickened me then, and I struggled to my feet and staggered back into the house without saying another word.

The effect of circumstances upon our own natures are forever springing surprises upon us. Within a few days I had acted the part of the hero of one of the Sunday School stories and taken my successful rival by the hand I suspect that after all I was a poor fire-eater after the first heat of resentment had been quenched, and far more suited to being the patient cripple (who dies scattering blessings and forgiveness) of the Misses Mainsleys' favourite Sabbath literature.

I was not so stubborn as to blind myself to the fact that Stephen was necessary to Beatrice's happiness, and I loved her well enough to pride myself upon it even yet. Her words, with the half-piteous, half-accusing ring, haunted my memory and made me feel a brute. 'You wouldn't like me to be miserable always, would you, Ned?' I fought and beat my own selfishness. I wanted Beatrice to be happy.

How seldom is the lover forced to admit that the affection of someone else for his mistress is stronger than his own! I tried to pretend that I cared more for Beatrice than ever Stephen could, and knew all the time that I was telling myself a lie. My love of her was the usual kind, half sentimental, half passionate. But theirs was different—how different I cannot explain. It was as if each saw in the other an ideal, the soul specially created by God to inspire and requite a perfect love. Such things have happened before in the world's history, and will happen again, until love goes the way of chivalry and all other good things.

It had made Stephen another man, or, rather it had changed him from a boy into a man. He had become serious and rather gloomy in contrast to his riotous joviality before he met Beatrice.

Those were terrible days for me. I won each of the terrible fights against my baser nature, but they were not bloodless victories. Yet I am glad now—glad to remember that afternoon when I joined hands with Stephen and Beatrice and promised to do my utmost to see them happily wedded. I see now that it was not so splendid as it seemed, that my generosity was to a great extent a pose; but I felt exalted and noble then, and Sidney Carton could not have been more pleased with himself I liked Stephen, and I know he came almost to worship me. He never quite forgave himself for nearly killing me that afternoon in the garden, and would hark back to the incident again and again, imploring my forgiveness. Once I questioned him about the peculiar and deadly hold he took upon my throat. I have already mentioned that he had seized my windpipe with the thumb and first finger of each hand, whereas most men would have gripped me with all their fingers.

'A gipsy showed me the hold,' he explained, it is the most deadly of all, provided you are strong in the thumb and finger. It's the same grip which Japanese dentists take upon their patients' teeth. You can choke a man in half the time that any other way would take.'

Pleasant as he was to talk with he had the temper of a devil when it was roused, and I was not comfortable in my mind as to the encounter between him and Lord Francis, which I was sure must come sooner or later. He told me that he made a practice of avoiding quarrels, knowing his dangerous and terrible failing, but he hated the sight of his rival, and I could not trust him to hold himself in check at any encounter between them.

Our greatest trouble in those days was old Martha, who was quick to see what had happened. She hated Stephen, and would scarcely speak to Beatrice, while as for me—'I've lost all patience with you, I have, Master Ned!' Poor old thing! We had trampled on her dreams and scored them with muddy footmarks. That Beatrice and I were no longer lovers was bad enough, but that I should stand by and even help my rival passed her comprehension. Her nature was free from all subtleties, and it was impossible to make her understand. More than once I had almost to go down on my knees to prevent her from betraying everything to the aunts. Looking back and joining together threads which escaped me at the time, I can see that Stephen and Beatrice suffered almost as much as I did. They were both beautiful characters and could not escape the pain they had caused me. I know that they were wonderfully considerate in my presence when I arranged meetings between them, and tried to behave as if the same comradeship existed between all three of us. They loved and admired me, too, and that helped me to hold my head up. Only Heaven and I know how near I often was to go whining to Beatrice's feet and beg her to take me back to her heart for the sake of the old, happy days.

There came at last an afternoon when Stephen, knowing his time to be short, went boldly to the aunts and asked for Beatrice's hand. I need not say what reception he met with, nor dwell angrily and contemptuously on the fact that Beatrice was imprisoned in her room for three days. Poor, simple old women, who tried to meddle with human souls, they loved Beatrice splendidly, and that was the only kind of love they knew.

To them, love was a thing indelicate except as between brothers and sisters and parents and children. Their ideas of marriage were strangely unbeautiful, thinking as they did that love ought not to exist between man and woman until the parson had mumbled the marriage service over them; and that if it did it was a shameful love. It was a comfortable creed to hold, for it excused a girl for accepting in a cold and businesslike way the offer of the most eligible man.

They thought seriously that no girl in her right mind could fail to be happy with a man like Lord Francis Brentford, and for Beatrice's own sake they pressed his suit with her. They were like the religious fanatics of olden times, who burned people's bodies in the earnest belief that they were saving the sufferers' souls.

A week later the war broke out, and Stephen's regiment was one of the first to be ordered to the Crimea.

On the night before he left us he came into the house wildly excited, with his eyes gleaming feverishly.

'I've managed to say goodbye to Beatrice,' he announced in a whisper, 'and—and I've met that swine Brentford again.'

I stared at him. 'You didn't quarrel?' I said in a halting voice.

'I didn't touch him,' he answered with queer emphasis. 'But, Ned, if you only knew how my fingers itched. The fool insulted me . . . madman! . . .I—I—it was for Beatrice's sake. I might have been a murderer, Ned, but I stood quite still, and my heart didn't quite burst. Look here!'

He showed me his hands. The balls of his thumbs and forefingers were quite flat, where he had pressed them together and imagined Lord Francis's throat between them. His palms were bleeding where he had dug his nails into them.

'What did you say?' I asked.

'I told him that Beatrice was mine and mine only; that if I came back and found that he had been troubling her I would kill him. He only laughed at that. Ned, I believe I ought to have killed him then!'

'Don't talk rubbish,' I said impatiently.

He sat down and rested his face between his hands.

'Oh, I don't know,' he muttered. 'If I killed him and got hanged for it we should both be out of the way. And you'd marry Beatrice. Yes you would, Ned. And you'd be happy, too, in time. Beatrice loves you, you know, in a sort of way. As it is I don't think any of us will ever be happy.'

I thought it a true prophecy, but tried to cheer him up. I promised that I would look after Beatrice while he was away, and do all I could in my small way to prevent the aunts from trying to rush her into a hasty marriage with his rival. When I said that he got up and held my hands for a long minute.

'You're the best fellow that ever lived,' he said. 'If I don't come back I hope you will make Beatrice happy.'

But I was happy already in a pleasant, melancholy way, for I saw myself alone on the heights, a picturesque figure of Tragedy looking sad and noble. Lord, how young I was! And yet the boy must have had some good in him. Next morning Stephen went away to join his regiment, and that was the last I saw of him, poor fellow.

When he had gone I felt like one who had awakened from a troublesome dream, the influence of which remained behind with the power to cast shadows and check laughter.

I was once more a frequent visitor at the House by the Crossroads, and Beatrice and I almost resumed the old life together. Still, it was not the same, and some ghost out of our childhood lurked for me in every familiar comer. But I was well content to be her friend, and have her near me, and sometimes a base hope that Stephen might desert her, or meet his death, would rise up in my mind and never allow itself to be utterly crushed. I was only human after all, and much more primitive than I knew.

I used to bring Beatrice the paper, having first looked to see that Stephen's name was not in the lists of killed and wounded, and we would read together the stories of marches and counter-marches, battles and skirmishes, and much patriotic talk of the might of British arms, and how soon the Russian bear must needs draw in his claws.

We had neither of us the faintest idea of the horrors of war. We never thought of living bodies lying disembowelled, or the horrors of cold and hunger. The dead, we fancied, died in a moment, and we imagined the wounded as suffering no more than a child with measles. To Beatrice the war was a sort of Astley's Circus in which Stephen was performing. She would not allow herself to think that he ran any risk of being killed.

So time passed pleasantly, if still a little sadly for me, until the day came when the definite announcement of Beatrice's engagement to Lord Francis Brentford gave me one of the greatest shocks I had ever experienced. I had not seen Beatrice for three days, and on the previous occasion of our meeting she had said nothing to me and seemed quite cheerful and hopeful of the future. A brief note, however, addressed to my father by Aunt Mary confirmed the report. I lost no time in hastening to see Beatrice. She was alone in the dining-room when I was ushered in. Her eyes were red with weeping and her cheeks were a ghastly grey. For the first time in her life she looked ugly, and her pretty hair was all draggled and untidy. She said nothing to me at first, but came and put her hands on my shoulders and cried with her face against my coat.

I held her tightly against me, with the old love of her burning fiercely in my heart. I, too, was broken and miserable, for a pedestal had slipped away and my own picturesque image lay shattered on the ground. I was no longer Tragedy enthroned, but poor old Ned once again—just Ned, the tame cat, who was there when he was wanted.

'You—you've heard?' she whispered brokenly at last.

I nodded, and looked away so that she should not see the bitterness in my face. All I had suffered had gone for nothing. I had made great sacrifices for Stephen, and they were all to be wasted.

'I had to do it,' she moaned. 'Aunt Mary told me that their allowance would stop unless I did, and I could not see them turned out in the street after all they've done for me. God knows I'd rather die, Ned. But—Stephen will understand.'

I doubted if Stephen would. I knew that Lord Francis would be a dead man immediately he returned. I imagined Stephen's face when he landed in England and heard the news, if, indeed, he was mercifully spared a letter in the trenches outside Sevastopol.

'Can't you hold out?' I groaned. 'Wait a little longer. The war may end suddenly and Stephen come back. Try to wait a little longer, Beatrice.'

She shook her head. 'I can do nothing if the aunts are to be saved. The wedding is fixed for a month from today.'

I pushed her gently from me, with an odd loyalty to Stephen stirring within me.

'I am going to see the aunts,' I said; and so quitted the room.

I saw them, and they listened to me while I raged, at first staring in mild surprise and then with wooden faces. When I ceased speaking they answered me with a gentle courtesy that almost touched me. They were older than I, Aunt Mary said, and they were Beatrice's aunts. They alone were capable of judging what was best for her.

I know now that they lied in their story of the allowance, but I cannot help knowing that they were good women, honest at least in purpose. One of the tragedies of life is that the good women do quite as much harm as the bad ones. Well, I had done my part, and I could do nothing more but look on, come to see Beatrice every day and try to cheer her, pray that something unforeseen would yet stop the marriage. Then, at last, came the eve of that marriage mockery, destined after all never to be performed.

That evening is as clear to my memory as the events of yesterday, and though what happened must be recorded it does not bear dwelling upon. I called to see Beatrice as usual, and old Martha came to the door with eyes red and swollen. The aunts, she said, wanted to see me, and she conducted me forthwith to the drawing-room.

The old ladies were sorely troubled about Beatrice for perhaps the first time since she had consented to marry her kinsman. About half an hour since, they told me, she had fainted dead away, and upon coming to had declared that Stephen was dead, and had broken out into an uncontrollable fit of weeping. She had gone to her room and was now quiet, but there was something in the calm that had come over her which they feared worse than her terrible outburst. She still adhered to her statement that Stephen was dead, but would not say how she knew. Could I see her and talk her into a reasonable frame of mind?

I felt myself turn white. A sudden fear was round my heart. I believed in Beatrice's presentiment, and I knew then that she, too, would die.

'It's all your fault,' was all I could find to say to the two poor ladies.

'All your fault!'

Before they could answer, a horseman rode up to the door. Lord Francis was stopping only six miles away, and the aunts knew who it was. I saw consternation on both their faces.

Aunt Jane ran to the door, and as Martha passed, she said, 'Show his lordship up to the library and say we will not keep him waiting a moment.'

'Something must be done with Beatrice before he sees her,' Aunt Jane whispered as we heard his heavy footsteps go past the door. 'Ned, dear boy, you are her friend. We will take you up to her and you must reason with her.

Tell her that she is being wickedly foolish—that there is no reason to suppose that any harm has befallen Lieutenant Burgess, that tomorrow she will be the wife of another man and has no right to worry about him.' I hesitated. I did not know what to say. I am not sure if I answered at all, for just then we heard another knock on the door, and we listened to hear Martha go through the hall and open it.

Then her scream rang sharp and ghastly through the house.

We looked at each other in silence, and then I crossed the room and flung open the door. I have a vague memory of hearing footsteps upon the stairs, but before I could be certain Martha had flung herself, half demented, into my arms.

'Mr Burgess!' she kept saying in a strained voice, that seemed to come from the back of her throat.

We gathered round her and all our voices raised at once broke out into a babble of which only stray words were distinguishable. And then I heard Martha's voice, clear above all the others.

'He went upstairs! He pushed past me and went upstairs! He was dressed like a soldier, and his chest was torn to pieces. There was blood all over his clothes and he looked at me—he looked at me—like—'

A cry from upstairs hushed her, and we stood still, with our warm breath going up through the cold air in little wavering trails of steam. The cry was followed by a heavy crash, and then the old house was as still as it is today. The aunts stood still in graven images, with lines of hideous fear seared deeply in their faces. Between them Martha crouched on the floor and gibbered. She begged me to run away with Miss Beatrice, and said that she had a hundred pounds saved up.

I went upstairs and into the library with terror clogging my feet, and there I found that same nightmare which I had dreamed and forgotten Heaven knows when had come true.

Lord Francis Brentford lay on the floor, his knees humped up, his arms spread out, and his fists clenched. His face was almost as black as a negro's, and on his throat were the marks of two thumbs and two fingers—blue and purple bruises—Stephen's marks!

I reeled and tripped over his body and fell fainting.

It was Aunt Jane who brought me to. She was nearly beside herself—nearly as mad as poor Martha had suddenly become. She told me that Martha had just seen Stephen and Beatrice leave the house together, he leading her by the hand.

It may have been true. Beatrice's spirit had certainly left the house. We went up together and found her lying on her bed all white and still. And Martha came up laughing at the top of her voice, and begged me to run away with her, and asked me to accept the hundred pounds that she had saved up. And there my memory fails me until some days later when I read in The Times what I already knew—that Stephen had been killed outside Sevastopol.

I am an old man now, and the story is almost forgotten, and most who hear it for the first time dismiss it with a laugh. But strange things happen at night in the House by the Crossroads, and nobody will live there except Wicks and his wife. And they would live in any house that has walls and roof.

Others are frightened by the noises that sometimes ring through the night, when phantom hoofs ring on the lonely road and the sob of a woman's broken heart goes out into the night—and again there are some who scoff at even their own fears, saying that what they hear is but the wail of the wind among the trees, the creak of rotting timber in the walls. It may be so. I can well believe that to the many only these material sounds can come; they are not tuned to the higher key needed to respond to that which is above things of the earth earthy, and of those who say they hear—such as Wicks and his wife—I often think they have heard the story and deceive themselves.

But granting all this, I know that to the chosen few those sounds are real, and my own old heart, with its still bitter ache, defies the passing of Time, living still, living ever in that far past that is still a fresh reality to me.

I have an odd thought that Heaven is no particular place, and that if I have earned any reward, the garden of the House by the Crossroads will be haunted too. But no one will fear the ghosts that will come to it, and folk passing by at night will stop and listen to two children laughing in a summer house long since rotted away.

When I go to join those I love the bitterness of death will be past, the sting of sorrow healed, and only tender memories remain of those who joyed and sorrowed, who lived and loved, hoped and feared, in the days when the last dead century was young.

How cold the room has grown . . .

Playmates

I

Although everybody who knew Stephen Everton agreed that he was the last man under Heaven who ought to have been allowed to bring up a child, it was fortunate for Monica that she fell into his hands; else she had probably starved or drifted into some refuge for waifs and strays. True her father, Sebastian Threlfall the poet, had plenty of casual friends. Almost everybody knew him slightly, and right up to the time of his final attack of delirium tremens he contrived to look one of the most interesting of the regular frequenters of the Cafe Royal. But people are generally not hasty to bring up the children of casual acquaintances, particularly when such children may be suspected of having inherited more than a fair share of human weaknesses.

Of Monica's mother literally nothing was known. Nobody seemed able to say if she were dead or alive. Probably she had long since deserted Threlfall for some consort able and willing to provide regular meals. Everton knew Threlfall no better than a hundred others knew him, and was ignorant of the daughter's existence until the father's death was a new topic of conversation in literary and artistic circles. People vaguely wondered what would become of 'the kid'; and while they were still wondering, Everton quietly took possession of her.

Who's Who will tell you the year of Everton's birth, the names of his Almae Matres (Winchester and Magdalen College, Oxford), the titles of his books and of his predilections for skating and mountaineering; but it is necessary to know the man a little less superficially. He was then a year or two short of fifty and looked ten years older. He was a tall, lean man, with a delicate pink complexion, an oval head, a Roman nose, blue eyes which looked out mildly through strong glasses, and thin straight lips drawn tightly over slightly protruding teeth. His high forehead was bare, for he was bald to the base of his skull. What remained of his hair was a neutral tint between black and grey, and was kept closely cropped. He contrived to look at once prim and irascible, scholarly and acute; Sherlock Holmes, perhaps, with a touch of old-maidishness.

The world knew him for a writer of books on historical crises. They were cumbersome books with cumbersome titles, written by a scholar for scholars. They brought him fame and not a little money. The money he could have afforded to be without, since he was modestly wealthy by inheritance. He was essentially a cold-blooded animal, a bachelor, a man of regular and temperate habits, fastidious, and fond of quietude and simple comforts.

Nobody is ever likely to know why Everton adopted the orphan daughter of a man whom he knew but slightly and neither liked nor respected. He was no lover of children, and his humours were sardonic rather than sentimental. I am only hazarding a guess when I suggest that, like so many childless men, he had theories of his own concerning the upbringing of children, which he wanted to see tested. Certain it is that Monica's childhood, which had been extraordinary enough before, passed from the tragic to the grotesque.

Everton took Monica from the Bloomsbury 'apartments' house, where the landlady, already nursing a bad debt, was wondering how to dispose of the child. Monica was then eight years old, and a woman of the world in her small way. She had lived with drink and poverty and squalor; had never played a game nor had a playmate; had seen nothing but the seamy side of life; and had learned skill in practising her father's petty shifts and mean contrivances. She was grave and sullen and plain and pale, this child who had never known childhood. When she spoke, which was as seldom as possible, her voice was hard and gruff. She was, poor little thing, as unattractive as her life could have made her.

She went with Everton without question or demur. She would no more have questioned anybody's ownership than if she had been an inanimate piece of luggage left in a cloak-room. She had belonged to her father. Now that he was gone to his own place she was the property of whomsoever chose to claim her. Everton took her with a cold kindness in which was neither love nor pity; in return she gave him neither love nor gratitude, but did as she was desired after the manner of a paid servant.

Everton disliked modem children, and for what he disliked in them he blamed modem schools. It may have been on this account that he did not send Monica to one; or perhaps he wanted to see how a child would contrive its own education. Monica could already read and write and, thus equipped, she had the run of his large library, in which was almost every conceivable kind of book from heavy tomes on abstruse subjects to trashy modem novels bought there and left by Miss Gribbin. Everton barred nothing, recommended nothing, but watched the tree grow naturally, untended and unpruned.

Miss Gribbin was Everton's secretary. She was the kind of hatchet-faced, flat-chested, middle-aged sexless woman who could safely share the home of a bachelor without either of them being troubled by the tongue of Scandal.

To her duties was now added the instruction of Monica in certain elementary subjects. Thus Monica learned that a man named William the Conqueror arrived in England in 1066; but to find out what manner of man this William was, she had to go to the library and read the conflicting accounts of him as given by the several historians. From Miss Gribbin she learned bare irrefutable facts; for the rest she was left to fend for herself. In the library she found herself surrounded by all the realms of reality and fancy, each with its door invitingly ajar.

Monica was fond of reading. It was, indeed, almost her only recreation, for Everton knew no other children of her age, and treated her as a grown-up member of the household. Thus she read everything from translations of the Iliad to Hans Andersen, from the Bible to the love-gush of the modem female fiction-mongers.

Everton, although he watched her closely, and plied her with innocent-sounding questions, was never allowed a peep into her mind. What muddled dreams she may have had of a strange world surrounding the Hampstead house—a world of gods and fairies and demons, and strong silent men making love to sloppy-minded young women—she kept to herself.

Reticence was all that she had in common with normal childhood, and Everton noticed that she never played.

Unlike most young animals, she did not take naturally to playing. Perhaps the instinct had been beaten out of her by the realities of life while her father was alive. Most lonely children improvise their own games and provide themselves with a vast store of make-believe. But Monica, as sullen-seeming as a caged animal, devoid alike of the naughtiness and the charms of childhood, rarely crying and still more rarely laughing, moved about the house sedate to the verge of being wooden. Occasionally Everton, the experimentalist, had twinges of conscience and grew half afraid . . .

II

When Monica was twelve Everton moved his establishment from Hampstead to a house remotely situated in the middle of Suffolk, which was part of a recent legacy. It was a tall, rectangular, Queen Anne house standing on a knoll above marshy fields and wind-bowed beech woods. Once it had been the manor house, but now little land went with it. A short drive passed between rank evergreens from the heavy wrought-iron gate to a circle of grass and flower beds in front of the house. Behind was an acre and a half of rank garden, given over to weeds and marigolds. The rooms were high and well lighted, but the house wore an air of depression as if it were a live thing unable to shake off some ancient fit of melancholy.

Everton went to live in the house for a variety of reasons. For the most part of a year he had been trying in vain to let or sell it, and it was when he found that he would have no difficulty in disposing of his house at Hampstead that he made up his mind. The old house, a mile distant from a remote Suffolk village, would give him all the solitude he required. Moreover he was anxious about his health—his nervous system had never been strong—and his doctor had recommended the bracing air of East Anglia.

He was not in the least concerned to find that the house was too big for him. His furniture filled the same number of rooms as it had filled at Hampstead, and the others he left empty. Nor did he increase his staff of three indoor servants and a gardener. Miss Gribbin, now less dispensable than ever, accompanied him; and with them came Monica to see another aspect of life, with the same wooden stoicism which Everton had remarked in her on the occasion of their first meeting.

As regarded Monica, Miss Gribbin's duties were then becoming more and more a sinecure. 'Lessons' now occupied no more than half-an-hour a day. The older Monica grew, the better she was able to grub for her education in the great library. Between Monica and Miss Gribbin there was neither love nor sympathy, nor was there any affectation of either. In their common duty to Everton they owed and paid certain duties to each other. Their intercourse began and ended there.

Everton and Miss Gribbin both liked the house at first. It suited the two temperaments which were alike in their lack of festivity. Asked if she too liked it, Monica said simply 'Yes', in a tone which implied stolid and complete indifference.

All three in their several ways led much the same lives as they had led in Hampstead. But a slow change began to work in Monica, a change so slight and subtle that weeks passed before Everton or Miss Gribbin noticed it. It was late on an afternoon in early spring when Everton first became aware of something unusual in Monica's demeanour.

He had been searching in the library for one of his own books—The Fall of the Commonwealth in England— and having failed to find it went in search of Miss Gribbin and met Monica instead at the foot of the long oak staircase. Of her he casually inquired about the book, and she jerked her head up brightly, to answer him with an unwonted smile:

'Yes, I've been reading it. I expect I left it in the schoolroom. I'll go and see.'

It was a long speech for her to have uttered, but Everton scarcely noticed that at the time. His attention was directed elsewhere.

'Where did you leave it?' he demanded.

'In the schoolroom,' she repeated.

'I know of no schoolroom,' said Everton coldly. He hated to hear anything mis-called, even were it only a room. 'Miss Gribbin generally takes you for your lessons in either the library or the dining-room. If it is one of those rooms, kindly call it by its proper name.'

Monica shook her head.

'No, I mean the schoolroom—the big empty room next to the library. That's what it's called.'

Everton knew the room. It faced north, and seemed darker and more dismal than any other room in the house. He had wondered idly why Monica chose to spend so much of her time in a room bare of furniture, with nothing better to sit on than uncovered boards or a cushionless window-seat; and put it down to her genius for being unlike anybody else.

'Who calls it that?' he demanded.

'It's its name,' said Monica, smiling.

She ran upstairs and presently returned with the book, which she handed to him with another smile. He was already wondering at her. It was surprising and pleasant to see her run, instead of the heavy and clumsy walk which generally moved her when she went to obey a behest. And she had smiled two or three times in the short space of a minute. Then he realized that for some little while she had been a brighter, happier creature than ever she had been at Hampstead.

'How did you come to call that room the schoolroom?' he asked, as he took the book from her hand.

'It is the schoolroom,' she insisted, seeking to cover her evasion by laying stress on the verb. That was all he could get out of her. As he questioned further the smiles ceased and the pale, plain little face became devoid of any expression. He knew then that it was useless to press her, but his curiosity was aroused. He inquired of Miss Gribbin and the servants, and learned that nobody was in the habit of calling the long, empty apartment the schoolroom.

Clearly Monica had given it its name. But why? She was so altogether remote from schools and schoolrooms. Some germ of imagination was active in her small mind. Everton's interest was stimulated. He was like a doctor who remarks in a patient some abnormal symptom.

'Monica seems a lot brighter and more alert than she used to be,' he remarked to Miss Gribbin.

'Yes,' agreed the secretary, 'I have noticed that. She is learning to play.'

'To play what? The piano?'

'No, no. To play childish games. Haven't you heard her dancing about and singing?'

Everton shook his head and looked interested.

'I have not,' he said. 'Possibly my presence acts as a check upon her—er—exuberance. '

'I hear her in that empty room which she insists upon calling the schoolroom. She stops when she hears my step. Of course, I have not interfered with her in any way, but I could wish that she would not talk to herself. I don't like people who do that. It is somehow— uncomfortable.'

'I didn't know she did,' said Everton slowly.

'Oh, yes, quite long conversations. I haven't actually heard what she talks about, but sometimes you would think that she was in the midst of a circle of friends.'

'In that same room?'

'Generally,' said Miss Gribbin, with a nod.

Everton regarded his secretary with a slow, thoughtful smile.

'Development,' he said, 'is always extremely interesting. I am glad the place seems to suit Monica. I think it suits all of us.'

There was a doubtful note in his voice as he uttered the last words, and Miss Gribbin agreed with him with the same lack of conviction in her tone. As a fact, Everton had been doubtful of late if his health had been benefited by the move from Hampstead. For the first week or two his nerves had been the better for the change of air; but now he was conscious of the beginning of a relapse. His imagination was beginning to play him tricks, filling his mind with vague, distorted fancies. Sometimes when he sat up late, writing—he was given to working at night on strong coffee—he became a victim of the most distressing nervous symptoms, hard to analyze and impossible to combat, which invariably drove him to bed with a sense of defeat.

That same night he suffered one of the variations of this common experience.

It was close upon midnight when he felt stealing over him a sense of discomfort which he was compelled to classify as fear. He was working in a small room leading out of the drawing-room which he had selected for his study. At first he was scarcely aware of the sensation. The effect was always cumulative; the burden was laid upon him straw by straw.

It began with his being oppressed by the silence of the house. He became more and more acutely conscious of it, until it became like a thing tangible, a prison of solid walls growing around him.

The scratching of his pen at first relieved the tension. He wrote words and erased them again for the sake of that comfortable sound. But presently that comfort was denied him, for it seemed to him that this minute and busy noise was attracting attention to himself. Yes, that was it. He was being watched.

Everton sat quite still, the pen poised an inch above the half-covered sheet of paper. This was become a familiar sensation. He was being watched. And by what? And from what corner of the room?

He forced a tremulous smile to his lips. One moment he called himself ridiculous; the next, he asked himself hopelessly how a man could argue with his nerves. Experience had taught him that the only cure—and that a temporary one—was to go to bed. Yet he sat on, anxious to learn more about himself, to coax his vague imaginings into some definite shape.

Imagination told him that he was being watched, and although he called it imagination he was afraid. That rapid beating against his ribs was his heart, warning him of fear. But he sat rigid, anxious to learn in what part of the room his fancy would place these imaginary 'watchers'—for he was conscious of the gaze of more than one pair of eyes being bent upon him. At first the experiment failed. The rigidity of his pose, the hold he was keeping upon himself, acted as a brake upon his mind. Presently he realized this and relaxed the tension, striving to give his mind that perfect freedom which might have been demanded by a hypnotist or one experimenting in telepathy.

Almost at once he thought of the door. The eyes of his mind veered around in that direction as the needle of a compass veers to the magnetic north. With these eyes of his imagination he saw the door. It was standing half open, and the aperture was thronged with faces. What kind of faces he could not tell. They were just faces; imagination left it at that. But he was aware that these spies were timid, that they were in some wise as fearful of him as he was of them; that to scatter them he had but to turn his head and gaze at them with the eyes of his body.

The door was at his shoulder. He turned his head suddenly and gave it one swift glance out of the tail of his eye.

However imagination deceived him, it had not played him false about the door. It was standing half open although he could have sworn that he had closed it on entering the room. The aperture was empty. Only darkness, solid as a pillar, filled the space between floor and lintel. But although he saw nothing as he turned his head, he was dimly conscious of something vanishing, a scurrying noiseless and incredibly swift, like the flitting of a trout in clear, shallow water.

Everton stood up, stretched himself, and brought his knuckles up to his strained eyes. He told himself that he must go to bed. It was bad enough that he must suffer these nervous attacks; to encourage them was madness. But as he mounted the stairs he was still conscious of not being alone. Shy, timorous, ready to melt into the shadows of the walls if he turned his head, They were following him, whispering noiselessly, linking hands and arms, watching him with the fearful, awed curiosity of—Children

III

The Vicar had called upon Everton. His name was Parslow, and he was a typical country parson of the poorer sort, a tall, rugged, shabby, worried man in the middle forties, obviously embarrassed by the eternal problem of making ends meet on an inadequate stipend.

Everton received him courteously enough, but with a certain coldness which implied that he had nothing in common with his visitor. Parslow was evidently disappointed because 'the new people' were not church-goers nor likely to take much interest in the parish. The two men made half-hearted and vain attempts to find common ground. It was not until he was on the point of leaving that the Vicar mentioned Monica.

'You have, I believe, a little girl?' he said.

'Yes. My small ward.'

'Ah! I expect she finds it lonely here. I have a little girl of the same age. She is at present away at school, but she will be home soon for the Easter holidays. I know she would be delighted if your little—er—ward would come down to the Vicarage and play with her sometimes.'

The suggestion was not particularly welcome to Everton, and his thanks were perfunctory. This other small girl, although she was a vicar's daughter, might carry the contagion of other modem children and infect Monica with the pertness and slanginess which he so detested. Altogether he was determined to have as little to do with the Vicarage as possible.

Meanwhile the child was becoming to him a study of more and more absorbing interest. The change in her was almost as marked as if she had just returned after having spent a term at school. She astonished and mystified him by using expressions which she could scarcely have learned from any member of the household. It was not the jargon of the smart young people of the day which slipped easily from her lips, but the polite family slang of his own youth. For instance, she remarked one morning that Mead, the gardener, was a whale at pruning vines.

A whale! The expression took Everton back a very long way down the level road of the spent years; took him, indeed, to a nursery in a solid respectable house in a Belgravian square, where he had heard the word used in that same sense for the first time. His sister Gertrude, aged ten, notorious in those days for picking up loose expressions, announced that she was getting to be a whale at French. Yes, in those days an expert was a 'whale' or a 'don'; not, as he is today, a 'stout fellow'. But who was a 'whale' nowadays? It was years since he had heard the term.

'Where did you learn to say that?' he demanded in so strange a tone that Monica stared at him anxiously.

'Isn't it right?' she asked eagerly. She might have been a child at a new school, fearful of not having acquired the fashionable phraseology of the place.

'It is a slang expression,' said the purist coldly. 'It used to mean a person who was proficient in something. How did you come to hear it?'

She smiled without answering, and her smile was mysterious, even coquettish after a childish fashion. Silence had always been her refuge, but it was no longer a sullen silence. She was changing rapidly, and in a manner to bewilder her guardian. He failed in an effort to cross-examine her, and, later in the day, consulted Miss Gribbin.

'That child,' he said, 'is reading something that we know nothing about.'

'Just at present,' said Miss Gribbin, 'she is glued to Dickens and Stevenson.'

'Then where on earth does she get her expressions?'

'I don't know,' the secretary retorted testily, 'any more than I know how she learned to play Cat's Cradle.'

'What? That game with string? Does she play that?'

'I found her doing something quite complicated and elaborate the other day. She wouldn't tell me how she learned to do it. I took the trouble to question the servants, but none of them had shown her.'

Everton frowned.

'And I know of no book in the library which tells how to perform tricks with string. Do you think she has made a clandestine friendship with any of the village children?'

Miss Gribbin shook her head.

'She is too fastidious for that. Besides, she seldom goes into the village alone.'

There, for the time, the discussion ended. Everton, with all the curiosity of the student, watched the child as carefully and closely as he was able without at the same time arousing her suspicions. She was developing fast. He had known that she must develop, but the manner of her doing so amazed and mystified him, and, likely as not, denied some preconceived theory. The untended plant was not only growing but showed signs of pruning. It was as if there were outside influences at work on Monica which could have come neither from him nor from any other member of the household.

Winter was dying hard, and dark days of rain kept Miss Gribbin, Monica and Everton within doors. He lacked no opportunities of keeping the child under observation, and once, on a gloomy afternoon, passing the room which she had named the schoolroom, he paused and listened until he became suddenly aware that his conduct bore an unpleasant resemblance to eavesdropping. The psychologist and the gentleman engaged in a brief struggle in which the gentleman temporarily got the upper hand. Everton approached the door with a heavy step and flung it open.

The sensation he received, as he pushed open the door, was vague but slightly disturbing, and it was by no means new to him. Several times of late, but generally after dark, he had entered an empty room with the impression that it had been occupied by others until the very moment of his crossing the threshold. His coming disturbed not merely one or two, but a crowd. He felt rather than heard them scattering, flying swiftly and silently as shadows to incredible hiding-places, where they held breath and watched and waited for him to go. Into the same atmosphere of tension he now walked, and looked about him as if expecting to see more than only the child who held the floor in the middle of the room, or some tell-tale trace of other children in hiding. Had the room been furnished he must have looked involuntarily for shoes protruding from under table or settees, for ends of garments unconsciously left exposed.

The long room, however, was empty save for Monica from wainscot to wainscot and from floor to ceiling. Fronting him were the long high window's starred by fine rain. With her back to the white filtered light Monica faced him, looking up to him as he entered. He was just in time to see a smile fading from her lips. He also saw by a slight convulsive movement of her shoulders that she was hiding something from him in the hands clasped behind her back.

'Hullo,' he said, with a kind of forced geniality, 'what are you up to?'

She said, 'Nothing', but not as sullenly as she would once have said it.

'Come,' said Everton, 'that is impossible. You were talking to yourself, Monica. You should not do that. It is an idle and a very, very foolish habit. You will go mad if you continue to do that.'

She let her head droop a little.

'I wasn't talking to myself,' she said in a low, half playful but very deliberate tone.

'That's nonsense. I heard you.'

'I wasn't talking to myself.'

'But you must have been. There is nobody else here.'

'There isn't—now.'

'What do you mean? Now?'

'They've gone. You frightened them, I expect.'

'What do you mean?' he repeated, advancing a step or two towards her.

'And whom do you call "they'?'

Next moment he was angry with himself. His tone was so heavy and serious and the child was half laughing at him. It was as if she were triumphant at having inveigled him into taking a serious part in her own game of make-believe.

'You wouldn't understand,' she said.

'I understand this—that you are wasting your time and being a very silly little girl. What's that you're hiding behind your back?'

She held out her right hand at once, unclenched her fingers and disclosed a thimble. He looked at it and then into her face.

'Why did you hide that from me?' he asked. 'There was no need.'

She gave him her faint secretive smile—that new smile of hers—before replying.

'We were playing with it. I didn't want you to know.'

'You were playing with it, you mean. And why didn't you want me to know?'

'About them. Because I thought you wouldn't understand. You don't understand. '

He saw that it was useless to affect anger or show impatience. He spoke to her gently, even with an attempt at displaying sympathy.

'Who are "they'?' he asked.

'They're just them. Other girls.'

'I see. And they come and play with you, do they? And they run away whenever I'm about, because they don't like me. Is that it?'

She shook her head.

'It isn't that they don't like you. I think they like everybody. But they're so shy. They were shy of me for a long, long time. I knew they were there, but it was weeks and weeks before they'd come and play with me. It was weeks before I even saw them.'

'Yes? Well, what are they like?'

'Oh, they're just girls. And they're awfully, awfully nice. Some are a bit older than me and some are a bit younger. And they don't dress like other girls you see today. They're in white with longer skirts and they wear sashes.'

Everton inclined his head gravely. 'She got that out of the illustrations of books in the library,' he reflected.

'You don't happen to know their names, I suppose?' he asked, hoping that no quizzical note in his voice rang through the casual but sincere tone which he intended.

'Oh, yes. There's Mary Hewitt—I think I love her best of all—and Elsie Power, and -'

'How many of them altogether?'

'Seven. It's just a nice number. And this is the schoolroom where we play games. I love games. I wish I'd learned to play games before.'

'And you've been playing with the thimble?'

'Yes. Hunt-the-thimble they call it. One of us hides it, and then the rest of us try to find it, and the one who finds it hides it again.'

'You mean you hide it yourself, and then go and find it.'

The smile left her face at once, and the look in her eyes warned him that she was done with confidences.

'Ah!' she exclaimed. 'You don't understand after all. I somehow knew you wouldn't.'

Everton, however, thought he did. His face wore a sudden smile of relief.

'Well, never mind,' he said. 'But I shouldn't play too much if I were you.'

With that he left her. But curiosity tempted him, not in vain, to linger and listen for a moment on the other side of the door which he had closed behind him. He heard Monica whisper, 'Mary! Elsie! Come on. It's all right. He's gone now.'

At an answering whisper, very unlike Monica's, he started violently and then found himself grinning at his own discomfiture. It was natural that Monica playing many parts, should try to change her voice with every character. He went downstairs sunk in a brown study which brought him to certain interesting conclusions. A little later he communicated these to Miss Gribbin.

'I've discovered the cause of the change in Monica. She's invented for herself some imaginary friends—other little girls, of course.'

Miss Gribbin started slightly and looked up from the newspaper which she had been reading.

'Really?' she exclaimed. 'Isn't that rather an unhealthy sign?'

'No, I should say not. Having imaginary friends is quite a common symptom of childhood, especially among young girls. I remember my sister used to have one, and was very angry when none of the rest of us would take the matter seriously. In Monica's case I should say it was perfectly normal—normal, but interesting. She must have inherited an imagination from that father of hers, with the result that she has seven imaginary friends, all properly named, if you please. You see, being lonely, and having no friends of her own age, she would naturally invent more than one "friend".

They are all nicely and primly dressed, I must tell you, out of Victorian books which she has found in the library.'

'It can't be healthy,' said Miss Gribbin, pursing her lips. 'And I can't understand how she has learned certain expressions and a certain style of talking and games'

'All out of books. And pretends to herself that "they" have taught her. But the most interesting part of the affair is this: it's given me my first practical experience of telepathy, of the existence of which I had hitherto been rather sceptical. Since Monica invented this new game, and before I was aware that she had done so, I have had at different times distinct impressions of there being a lot of little girls about the house.'

Miss Gribbin started and stared. Her lips parted as if she were about to speak, but it was as if she had changed her mind while framing the first word she had been about to utter.

'Monica,' he continued smiling, 'invented these "friends", and has been making me telepathetically aware of them, too. I have lately been most concerned about the state of my nerves.'

Miss Gribbin jumped up as if in anger, but her brow was smooth and her mouth dropped at the comers.

'Mr Everton,' she said, 'I wish you had not told me all this.' Her lips worked. 'You see,' she added unsteadily, 'I don't believe in telepathy.'

IV

Easter, which fell early that year, brought little Gladys Parslow home for the holidays to the Vicarage. The event was shortly afterwards signalized by a note from the Vicar to Everton, inviting him to send Monica down to have tea and play games with his little daughter on the following Wednesday.

The invitation was an annoyance and an embarrassment to Everton. Here was the disturbing factor, the outside influence, which might possibly thwart his experiment in the upbringing of Monica. He was free, of course, simply to decline the invitation so coldly and briefly as to make sure that it would not be repeated; but the man was not strong enough to stand on his own feet impervious to the winds of criticism. He was sensitive and had little wish to seem churlish, still less to appear ridiculous. Taking the line of least resistance he began to reason that one child, herself no older than Monica, and in the atmosphere of her own home, could make little impression. It ended in his allowing Monica to go.

Monica herself seemed pleased at the prospect of going but expressed her pleasure in a discreet, restrained, grown-up way. Miss Gribbin accompanied her as far as the Vicarage doorstep, arriving with her punctually at half-past three on a sullen and muggy afternoon, and handed her over to the woman-of-all-work who answered the summons at the door.

Miss Gribbin reported to Everton on her return. An idea which she conceived to be humorous had possession of her mind, and in talking to Everton she uttered one of her infrequent laughs.

'I only left her at the door,' she said, 'so I didn't meet the other little girl. I wish I'd stayed to see that. It must have been funny.'

She irritated Everton by speaking exactly as if Monica were a captive animal which had just been shown, for the first time in its life, another of its own kind. The analogy thus conveyed to Everton was close enough to make him wince. He felt something like a twinge of conscience, and it may have been then that he asked himself for the first time if he were being fair to Monica.

It had never once occurred to him to ask himself if she were happy. The truth was that he understood children so little as to suppose that physical cruelty was the one kind of cruelty from which they were capable of suffering. Had he ever before troubled to ask himself if Monica were happy, he had probably given the question a curt dismissal with the thought that she had no right to be otherwise. He had given her a good home, even luxuries, together with every opportunity to develop her mind. For companions she had himself, Miss Gribbin, and, to a limited extent, the servants. . . .

Ah, but that picture, conjured up by Miss Gribbin's words with their accompaniment of unreasonable laughter! The little creature meeting for the first time another little creature of its own kind and looking bewildered, knowing neither what to do nor what to say. There was pathos in that—uncomfortable pathos for Everton. Those imaginary friends—did they really mean that Monica had needs of which he knew nothing, of which he had never troubled to learn?

He was not an unkind man, and it hurt him to suspect that he might have committed an unkindness. The modem children whose behaviour and manners he disliked, were perhaps only obeying some inexorable law of evolution. Suppose in keeping Monica from their companionship he were actually flying in the face of Nature? Suppose, after all, if Monica were to be natural, she must go unhindered on the tide of her generation?

He compromised with himself, pacing the little study. He would watch Monica much more closely, question her when he had the chance. Then, if he found she was not happy, and really needed the companionship of other children, he would see what could be done.

But when Monica returned home from the Vicarage it was quite plain that she had not enjoyed herself. She was subdued, and said very little about her experience. Quite obviously the two little girls had not made very good friends. Questioned, Monica confessed that she did not like Gladys—much. She said this very thoughtfully with a little pause before the adverb.

'Why don't you like her?' Everton demanded bluntly.

'I don't know. She's so funny. Not like other girls.'

'And what do you know about other girls?' he demanded, faintly amused.

'Well, she's not a bit like'

Monica paused suddenly and lowered her gaze.

'Not like your "friends", you mean?' Everton asked. She gave him a quick, penetrating little glance and then lowered her gaze once more.

'No,' she said, 'not a bit.'

She wouldn't be, of course. Everton teased the child with no more questions for the time being, and let her go. She ran off at once to the great empty room, there to seek that uncanny companionship which had come to suffice her.

For the moment Everton was satisfied. Monica was perfectly happy as she was, and had no need of Gladys, or, probably, any other child friends. His experiment with her was shaping successfully. She had invented her own young friends, and had gone off eagerly to play with the creations of her own fancy.

This seemed very well at first. Everton reflected that it was just what he would have wished, until he realized suddenly with a little shock of discomfort that it was not normal and it was not healthy.

V

Although Monica plainly had no great desire to see any more of Gladys Parslow, common civility made it necessary for the vicar's little daughter to be asked to pay a return visit. Most likely Gladys Parslow was as unwilling to come as was Monica to entertain her. Stem discipline, however, presented her at the appointed time on an afternoon pre-arranged by correspondence, when Monica received her coldly and with dignity, tempered by a sort of grown-up graciousness.

Monica bore her guest away to the big empty room, and that was the last of Gladys Parslow seen by Everton or Miss Gribbin that afternoon. Monica appeared alone when the gong sounded for tea, and announced in a subdued tone that Gladys had already gone home.

'Did you quarrel with her?' Miss Gribbin asked quickly.

'No—o.'

'Then why has she gone like this?'

'She was stupid,' said Monica, simply. 'That's all.'

'Perhaps it was you who was stupid. Why did she go?'

' She got frightened. '

'Frightened!'

'She didn't like my friends.'

Miss Gribbin exchanged glances with Everton.

'She didn't like a silly little girl who talks to herself and imagines things. No wonder she was frightened. '

'She didn't think they were real at first, and laughed at me,' said Monica, sitting down.

'Naturally!'

'And then when she saw them'

Miss Gribbin and Everton interrupted her simultaneously, repeating in unison and with well-matched astonishment, her last two words.

'And then when she saw them,' Monica continued unperturbed, 'she didn't like it. I think she was frightened. Anyhow, she said she wouldn't stay and went straight off home. I think she's a stupid girl. We all had a good laugh about her after she was gone. '

She spoke in her ordinary matter-of-fact tones, and if she were secretly pleased at the state of perturbation into which her words had obviously thrown Miss Gribbin she gave no sign of it. Miss Gribbin immediately exhibited outward signs of anger.

'You are a very naughty child to tell such untruths. You know perfectly well that Gladys couldn't have seen your "friends". You have simply frightened her by pretending to talk to people who weren't there, and it will serve you right if she never comes to play with you again.'

'She won't,' said Monica. 'And she did see them, Miss Gribbin.'

'How do you know?' Everton asked.

'By her face. And she spoke to them too, when she ran to the door. They were very shy at first because Gladys was there. They wouldn't come for a long time, but I begged them, and at last they did.'

Everton checked another outburst from Miss Gribbin with a look. He wanted to learn more, and to that end he applied some show of patience and gentleness.

'Where did they come from?' he asked. 'From outside the door?'

'Oh, no. From where they always come.'

'And where's that?'

'I don't know. They don't seem to know themselves. It's always from some direction where I'm not looking. Isn't it strange?'

'Very! And do they disappear in the same way?'

Monica frowned very seriously and thoughtfully.

'It's so quick you can't tell where they go. When you or Miss Gribbin come in—'

'They always fly on our approach, of course. But why?'

'Because they're dreadfully, dreadfully shy. But not so shy as they were. Perhaps soon they'll get used to you and not mind at all.'

'That's a comforting thought!' said Everton with a dry laugh.

When Monica had taken her tea and departed, Everton turned to his secretary.

'You are wrong to blame the child. These creations of her fancy are perfectly real to her. Her powers of suggestion have been strong enough to force them to some extent on me. The little Parslow girl, being younger and more receptive, actually sees them. It is a clear case of telepathy and auto-suggestion. I have never studied such matters, but I should say that these instances are of some scientific interest.'

Miss Gribbin's lips tightened and he saw her shiver slightly.

'Mr Parslow will be angry,' was all she said.

'I really cannot help that. Perhaps it is all for the best. If Monica does not like his little daughter they had better not be brought together again.'

For all that, Everton was a little embarrassed when on the following morning he met the vicar out walking. If the Rev. Parslow knew that his little daughter had left the house so unceremoniously on the preceding day, he would either wish to make an apology or perhaps require one, according to his view of the situation. Everton did not wish to deal in apologies one way or the other, he did not care to discuss the vagaries of children, and altogether he wanted to have as little to do with Mr Parslow as was conveniently possible. He would have passed with a brief acknowledgement of the vicar's existence, but, as he had feared, the vicar stopped him. 'I had been meaning to come and see you,' said the Rev. Parslow. Everton halted and sighed inaudibly, thinking that perhaps this casual meeting out of doors might after all have saved him something.

'Yes?' he said.

'I will walk in your direction if I may.' The vicar eyed him anxiously.

'There is something you must certainly be told. I don't know if you guess, or if you already know. If not, I don't know how you will take it. I really don't.'

Everton looked puzzled. Whichever child the vicar might blame for the hurried departure of Gladys, there seemed no cause for such a portentous face and manner.

'Really?' he asked. 'Is it something serious?'

'I think so, Mr Everton. You are aware, of course, that my little girl left your house yesterday afternoon with some lack of ceremony.'

'Yes, Monica told us she had gone. If they could not agree it was surely the best thing she could have done, although it may sound inhospitable of me to say it. Excuse me, Mr Parslow, but I hope you are not trying to embroil me in a quarrel between children?'

The vicar stared in his turn.

'I am not,' he said, 'and I am unaware that there was any quarrel. I was going to ask you to forgive Gladys. There was some excuse for her lack of ceremony. She was badly frightened, poor child.'

'Then it is my turn to express regret. I had Monica's version of what happened. Monica has been left a great deal to her own resources, and, having no playmates of her own age, she seems to have invented some.'

'Ah!' said the Rev. Parslow, drawing a deep breath.

'Unfortunately,' Everton continued, 'Monica has an uncomfortable gift for impressing her fancies on other people. I have often thought I felt the presence of children about the house, and so, I am almost sure, has Miss Gribbin. I am afraid that when your little girl came to play with her yesterday afternoon, Monica scared her by introducing her invisible "friends" and by talking to imaginary and therefore invisible little girls. '

The vicar laid a hand on Everton's arm.

'There is something more in it than that. Gladys is not an imaginative child; she is, indeed, a practical little person. I have never yet known her to tell me a lie. What would you say, Mr Everton, if I were to tell you that Gladys positively asserts that she saw those other children?'

Something like a cold draught went through Everton. An ugly suspicion, vague and almost shapeless, began to move in dim recesses of his mind. He tried to shake himself free of it, to smile and to speak lightly.

'I shouldn't be in the least surprised. Nobody knows the limits of telepathy and auto-suggestion. If I can feel the presence of children whom Monica has created out of her own imagination, why shouldn't your daughter, who is probably more receptive and impressionable than I am, be able to see them?'

The Rev. Parslow shook his head.

'Do you really mean that?' he asked. 'Doesn't it seem to you a little far-fetched?'

'Everything we don't understand must seem far-fetched. If one had dared to talk of wireless thirty years ago'

'Mr Everton, do you know that your house was once a girls' school?'

Once more Everton experienced that vague feeling of discomfiture.

'I didn't know,' he said, still indifferently.

'My aunt, whom I never saw, was there. Indeed she died there. There were seven who died. Diphtheria broke out there many years ago. It ruined the school which was shortly afterwards closed. Did you know that, Mr Everton? My aunt's name was Mary Hewitt'

'Good God!' Everton cried out sharply. 'Good God!'

'Ah!' said Parslow. 'Now do you begin to see?'

Everton, suddenly a little giddy, passed a hand across his forehead.

'That is—one of the names Monica told me,' he faltered. 'How could she know?'

'How indeed? Mary Hewitt's great friend was Elsie Power. They died within a few hours of each other.'

'That name too . . . she told me . . . and there were seven. How could she have known? Even the people around here wouldn't have remembered names after all these years. '

'Gladys knew them. But that was only partly why she was afraid. Yet I think she was more awed than afraid, because she knew instinctively that the children who came to play with little Monica, although they were not of this world, were good children, blessed children.'

'What are you telling me?' Everton burst out.

'Don't be afraid, Mr Everton. You are not afraid, are you? If those whom we call dead still remain close to us, what more natural than these children should come back to play with a lonely little girl who lacked human playmates? It may seem inconceivable, but how else explain it? How could little Monica have invented those two names? How could she have learned that seven little girls once died in your house? Only the very old people about here remember it, and even they could not tell you how many died or the name of any one of the little victims. Haven't you noticed a change in your ward since first she began to—imagine them, as you thought?'

Everton nodded heavily.

'Yes,' he said, almost unwittingly, 'she learned all sorts of tricks of speech, childish gestures which she never had before, and games...I couldn't understand. Mr Parslow, what in God's name am I to do?'

The Rev. Parslow still kept a hand on Everton's arm.

'If I were you I should send her off to school. It may not be very good for her.'

'Not good for her! But the children, you say '

'Children? I might have said angels. They will never harm her. But Monica is developing a gift of seeing and conversing with—with beings that are invisible and inaudible to others. It is not a gift to be encouraged. She may in time see and converse with others—wretched souls who are not God's children. She may lose the faculty if she mixes with others of her age. Out of her need I am sure, these came to her.'

'I must think,' said Everton. He walked on dazedly, in a moment or two the whole aspect of life had changed, had grown clearer, as if he had been blind from birth and was now given the first glimmerings of light. He looked forward no longer into the face of a blank and featureless wall, but through a curtain beyond which life manifested itself vaguely but at least perceptibly. His footfalls on the ground beat out the words: 'There is no death. There is no death.'

VI

That evening after dinner he sent for Monica and spoke to her in an unaccustomed way. He was strangely shy of her, and his hand, which he rested on one of her slim shoulders, lay there awkwardly.

'Do you know what I'm going to do with you, young woman?' he said. 'I'm going to pack you off to school.'

'O—oh!' she stared at him, half smiling 'Are you really?'

'Do you want to go?'

She considered the matter, frowning and staring at the tips of her fingers.

'I don't know. I don't want to leave them.'

'Who?' he asked.

'Oh, you know!' she said, and turned her head half shyly.

'What? Your—friends, Monica?'

'Yes.'

'Wouldn't you like other playmates?'

'I don't know. I love them, you see. But they said—they said I ought to go to school if you ever sent me. They might be angry with me if I was to ask you to let me stay. They wanted me to play with other girls who aren't—who aren't like they are. Because you know, they are different from children that everybody can see. And Mary told me not to—not to encourage anybody else who was different, like them.'

Everton drew a deep breath.

'We'll have a talk tomorrow about finding a school for you, Monica,' he said. 'Run off to bed, now. Goodnight, my dear.'

He hesitated, then touched her forehead with his lips. She ran from him, nearly as shy as Everton himself, tossing back her long hair, but from the door she gave him the strangest little brimming glance, and there was that in her eyes which he had never seen before.

Late that night Everton entered the great empty room which Monica had named the schoolroom. A flag of moonlight from the window lay across the floor, and it was empty to the gaze. But the deep shadows hid little shy presences of which some unnamed and undeveloped sense in the man was acutely aware.

'Children!' he whispered. 'Children!'

He closed his eyes and stretched out his hands. Still they were shy and held aloof, but he fancied that they came a little nearer.

'Don't be afraid,' he whispered. 'I'm only a very lonely man. Be near me after Monica is gone.'

He paused, waiting. Then as he turned away he was aware of little caressing hands upon his arm. He looked around at once, but the time had not yet come for him to see. He saw only the barred window, the shadows on either wall and the flag of moonlight.

The Summer-House

It is only fair to warn the unwary that this is an unsatisfactory sort of story, lacking in that completeness which, nowadays, is considered good money's worth. But I do not consider it my business to fill up the spaces between the lines. They are open to those who care to read.

Oliver was a stout young fellow of five when the family moved to Bitteme Hillside. The family consisted of himself and his father and mother, together with Annie, his nurse, and two more female servants. The small staff of servants was almost immediately increased to eight, including a middle-aged gentleman of magnificent presence, who now answered the front-door bell instead of Mary; for Mr Fowler had recently made money in leather.

Mr Fowler, Oliver's father, was middle-aged and lean and bald, and through long association with leather had grown to look a little like the foundation of his fortune, after the same subtle fashion that some people come to resemble their domestic pets. Mrs Fowler was colourless and stupid, one of Nature's nonentities. She had met before moving to Bitteme Hillside three titled women, all wives of City knights, and found occasion to mention their names at every tea-party. These brief details are given to show that young Oliver, if he were unduly imaginative, did not owe it to immediate heredity.

Probably he enjoyed more than anybody else the move to Bitteme Hillside from the conventionality of Upper Norwood. His father wanted to impress his City friends by mentioning that he was now a country squire. His mother intended to storm what she described as County Society. They both had their disappointments; not so Oliver. To his eyes the long red-brick Queen Anne house with its beautiful simplicity of architecture was a palace out of one of the fairy stories which were occasionally read to him. The gardens, the small ring park, the model farm, the friendly cattle that grazed on 'Daddy's estate', were all to him in their several ways more splendid than anything he had previously seen, even on his annual visit to the seaside. Afterwards, when custom had stalled much, he was left with an abiding love for Bitteme Hillside, as if his forefathers for many generations had lived and died there.

The new home, where one could get lost at first even without wanting to, was a heaven-devised place for pastimes like hide-and-seek when Annie could be made skittish enough to play a real game with him. But he had not so poverty-stricken a mind as to be unable to find amusement for himself when left alone. He had the space now to play at being the hero of every story he knew, and he began to develop an affection for parts of the house and grounds, much as a cat might. For some unexplained reason he loved the cedar tree in the garden behind the house—thenceforward not to be called the back-garden, as savouring of commonness. But his favourite spot and place of retreat was the summer-house.

This little house, with tiled floor and lattice walls supported by pillars, was in the most secluded part of that garden which daddy and mummy did not like to hear called the back-garden. Oliver spent much of his time there when left to himself, with toys and picture-books. The truth was, although he did not realize it at first, he did not feel so lonely in the summer-house.

It was about this time, shortly after his arrival in Bitteme Hillside, that he began to have dreams, formless and incoherent to his waking memory. In them, or rather after them, he was conscious of loving something feminine which was neither his mother nor Annie. Both his mother and Annie he loved, but secretly deplored in both a lack of responsiveness. Certainly his mother kissed him once or twice a day, and even picked him up and nursed him uncomfortably in the presence of visitors, but he was old enough now to detect and resent theatricals. Annie made no pretences at all. It was her duty to look after him, and she did it grudgingly. Her favourite expressions were 'Bless the boy!' and 'Drat the child!' and her flat, red hand could sting when exasperation drove her to use it. Her round, vividly-coloured face, which invariably smelt of yellow soap, was, somehow, unsatisfactory to kiss.

Yes, that was the truth. His mother and Annie were both, in their different ways, unsatisfactory to kiss. His mother's cheeks were flaccid and nearly always cold, her lips were hardened by some preparation which made them look red. And yet he began to be conscious of the beauty and freshness of young girlhood, and of somebody loving him as he wanted to be loved. He had met no girls who were grown-up or nearly grown-up. Perhaps, one might suggest, his busy little mind had materialized her out of some picture once seen and subsequently forgotten. Perhaps he had already created the ideal, of which, during his adolescence, he was to go vainly in search

However that may be, he was conscious of a friendship, the incidents of which always just eluded his memory. He knew that sometimes he was drawn into a heaven of warm arms, and fresh girlish kisses covered his upturned face. Somehow, he could not remember her face—only just in glimpses which went out like sparks. And there was a fragrance about her, too—like a summer garden at night after a shower of rain.

It was all very puzzling to his small mind. He knew that he was not remembering somebody he had known when he was very little, for these vague impressions had not started until he came to Bitteme Hillside. The experiences were recent and continuous; he knew that they would go on happening. Having nobody in whom he felt that he could confide, he hugged these vague memories to himself. It was his secret, a rather jolly secret, but, at the same time, a bit 'scary'. It made one go a bit chilly and caused one's eyes to water when one thought of it. For although he knew that he had nothing to fear, he was well aware that this friend did not belong to the same world as Mummy and Annie.

It would be hard to say when he first began to associate his 'friend' with the summer-house. Something drew him there to play, and gradually he realized that he was not playing alone. This feeling was very nice at first, until he stopped playing and began to think about it. Then it seemed all wrong that there should be somebody there whom he couldn't see. At that he would take fright, like some little wild thing at the sound of a man's footstep, and run panic-stricken through the thicket to the friendly cedar on the lawn, which was overlooked by the long row of windows at the back of the house. The cedar was always 'home' when Annie played one of her rare games of hide-and-seek with him. It was 'home', too, in this queer game—which was something more than a game—that he played by himself.

But this was not the only sort of experience with which the summer-house provided him. Sometimes he felt the presence of two people there—two people who were tremendously real except that he could not see nor hear nor touch them. He was not more afraid on those occasions than on the others, although he always left more quickly. He knew, although panic hastened his little legs through the thicket, that nobody wanted to hurt him.

The sensation was the same that he experienced in the presence of grown-ups who wanted him to go so that they could talk in private. Being a sensitive little boy he was quick to detect when his father and mother wanted to talk privately, and knew instinctively when they were going to tell him to 'ran and find Annie'.

At five or six years old one learns things without realising them. Instinct is there without much development of reasoning. Thus he discovered, without thinking it strange, that if Annie or any other grown-up accompanied him to the summer-house there was never any other presence there.

Once, when his father brought two noisy City gentlemen home for the week-end, they spent the whole of Sunday afternoon there, with cigars and funny-shaped bottles which contained vividly-coloured medicines. They had Oliver with them for a little while, and although they called him Old Chap, and enriched him by tossing him for pennies, he was resentful of their presence and went to sulk for the rest of the afternoon under the cedar. He was well aware that they had driven Her away. He did not mind their having driven away That Other who was sometimes with Her in the summer-house. He was jealous of Him. When He was there She was a grown-up and did not desire the presence of little boys. Somehow, he was sure that That Other was male, just as he knew that She was female. But the male presence, while he disliked it, was very dim to his perception.

Without Hers he would not have noticed it at all.

During the long months which intervened before he arrived at the age of six he longed for somebody whom he could make a confidant, although, if he found one, he was miserably aware that he could not make himself understood. Grown-ups sometimes failed to understand him when he tried to explain the simplest things.

Mr Beale, who answered the front-door bell and waited at table, and knew what was going to win a race which he called the 'Durby', was the most consistently friendly and cheerful of the mortals with whom he came in contact. But instinct made him doubt Mr Beale's ability to grasp the situation. He was quite sure that Mr Beale would only whistle.

Mummy, daddy, and Annie were quite out of the question. He placed them in the same mental category as Mr Beale. Besides—and here caution whispered at his elbow—this was a direct way to getting the summer-house put out of bounds. Experience had taught him that the things he liked doing most were forbidden as soon as detected.

But although he would not tell anybody exactly what was in his small mind, he developed cunning and began to fish for information. This was not easy, for grown-ups detested to be asked irrelevant questions. But on his sixth birthday, when even Annie had to affect good humour with him, he took advantage of the occasion.

'Please, Annie, can you dream about what isn't really there?'

'Of course you can,' said Annie briefly.

He was sure she had not understood.

'Sometimes,' he explained, 'I dream about you and daddy and mummy. But you're really there. Well, can you dream about anybody who isn't there at all?'

'Of course you can,' said Annie. 'Why, I dreamed of a big monkey the other night.'

'But there are big monkeys.'

'Nothing like the one I dreamed about,' said Annie definitely. 'At least,' she added, with a reminiscent shiver, 'I 'ope to 'eaven there isn't! Why, what have you been dreaming, Master Oliver?'

But Oliver had learned all he wanted to know for the time being. To say another word about dreams might cause the curtailment of his supper and possibly hasten his bed-time. He had learned caution. But his heart was heavy within him, and when Annie's back was turned he ran off to cry under the friendly cedar.

So perhaps She wasn't real, after all—only just a make-believe, the lovely, pretty lady who brought love and warmth and colour and perfume into his dreams.

But next morning he woke comforted, with more dim and rapidly-fading memories, and warm as if fresh from the embrace of Her enfolding arms. When Oliver was six and a half his education began in earnest, and he was promoted to having a governess. Annie, who was a good needlewoman, and had been learning the arts and crafts of a lady's maid, became the personal attendant of his mother.

Miss Cartwright, who had been strongly recommended by Lady Somebody, was middle-aged, conscientious and efficient. She was not the sort of person to inspire affection in Oliver, but she did inspire trust, and she had the knack of understanding children.

Yet Oliver never told her about his dreams, or of the invisible people who came to the summer-house when he was there. She was too hard and practical to invite a confidence of that sort. For the dreams, which left only thin wavering traces of memory behind them, still continued, and the summer-house was still a place of delight, of awe, and sometimes of fear. Oliver only remembered fragments of his dreams until something in real life sharply reminded him of something that came into them.

One evening, at half-past seven, the usual hour of his bed-time, mummy was dressing for dinner. There were to be several guests that night, and she was making a more than usually elaborate toilet. Generally, she did not change her frock till after he had gone to bed, but tonight he was told to go to her room and say goodnight to her.

Annie was brushing her hair when he arrived, and the dress she was to wear was laid out for her on the bed. 'The colour was peacock-blue, and more suitable for a young girl. Instantly it attracted Oliver's gaze. For him the bright lights blazing on the silver of the dressing-table shone in vain. He stood staring, and uttered two little quick gasps. It was the colour She wore, but in his waking life he had not known it until now.

'What's the matter?' his mother asked indifferently. 'Have you been running upstairs? Come and kiss me goodnight.'

He went towards her uncertainly, glancing back over his shoulder at the dress. Then, as his face drew close to that of the woman in the chair, he uttered a little sobbing cry, and clung to her.

'Mummy, mummy!' he cried. 'The scent! The scent!'

Mrs Fowler had liberally anointed herself with White Heather. She had never used it before, but Oliver recognized it. One may be mistaken over many things, but not over scent. Nothing is quicker or more certain to awaken memory.

'Well, I never!' exclaimed Annie.

'You funny boy!' laughed Mrs Fowler. 'Don't you like it?'

But he clung to her tenaciously, sobbing. He was frightened without knowing what made him afraid. That scent of White Heather was part of Her. She wore a dress of that funny sort of blue. Bit by bit he was going to remember her. Bit by bit he was going to see her.

He longed then to tell his mother everything, only what was there to tell? Mummy would not believe, or understand. Besides, it wasn't as if he wasn't awfully fond of Her. He was; only he was afraid.

'He was just like that before he had measles, m'm,' said Annie, when Oliver had been chided and sent away.

Not long after that came the climax. Looking back on it from his maturity Oliver was aware that he knew even then that it must come, and that he himself would bring it about.

He was getting a big boy now in his own estimation. He bathed and dressed himself, and was old enough to resent it when Philistines addressed him as 'little man'. Jerry, the second-gardener, bowled to him with a hard ball, and he could ride his pony without anybody leading it. He was beginning to think that Master Oliver Fowler was a person of some consequence.

On a certain warm, sunny afternoon he took with him to the summer-house a box containing his new train, set of rails, station, arch, and signal. The train when wound up went round and round in a series of circles, and it was fascinating to see if one could so wind it as to make it stop at the station without checking it by hand. He was so engaged when the old sensation stole over him. She was there, and not only She but He as well.

The old feeling of awe passed over him as he turned the key which wound up the spring.

He watched the train spin round and round, past the station, and through the arch. Three, four, five times round it went before its speed slackened, and it came to a halt, and he knew that other eyes watched it besides his own. That miserable snubbed feeling of being a little boy who was in the way overtook him, as it always did when He was there.

He was jealous and sulky, besides being awe-stricken. It was only when He was there that She wanted him to go. Well, this time he just wasn't going. He glowered defiance at the seats, which looked empty to his eyes, as once more he turned the key.

Off went the train once more on its monotonous journey. His gaze followed it while his lips pouted sullenly. The snubbed, hurt feeling grew and grew. He had never felt it so strongly before, except when a favourite aunt had told him that little boys who were gentlemen did not remain in the room when their elders wanted to talk.

'I don't care!' he said aloud. 'I'm not going! I'm not going!'

The train stopped, and he wound it up again, only this time he did not look towards the seats. He kept his eyes on the train, and on the shining circle of aluminium rails. The straining engine sped from his hand once more.

Then he felt his heart beating violently. Terror, a lurking beast, leapt out upon him from some ambush of the mind—terror such as he had never felt before. Time seemed to have slowed down so that moments stretched themselves into minutes. The whirring toy crawled instead of sped. He watched it in nightmare panic—watched it because he dared not lift his eyes.

Never before had he felt Their presence so keenly; never before had They seemed so real. Even when he had run frightened from the summer-house he had not expected to see Them with his naked eyes. Now he knew that one glance over his shoulder would reveal Them to him. They meant him no harm, but now that he had defied Their wish that he should go, They were there in some new and dreadful sense of being present. Between past experiences and this there was all the difference of shadow and substance. This time They were there to be seen, and he would rather have died than see Them.

For long moments he stood sweating, panting, sobbing, the spell of terror holding his feet to the floor, while the toy-train completed half a dozen circles. The sound of it stopping acted like some sound which breaks the spell of a nightmare. He clapped his hands to his eyes, uttered one long cry, and blundered out, striking his head against one of the pillars as he went. Half stunned, he could still run. Twice he fell, tripping over the roots of trees, but both times he picked himself up and ran the faster.

Miss Cartwright was reading a book in the shade of the cedar on the lawn when a little boy, with a chalk-white face, a cut forehead, and a smear of blood on his cheek, flung himself sobbing into the sanctuary of her arms, and buried his face in her lap.

'They're there! I nearly saw them. Oh, don't let me see them!' was all that she could get from him at first, and, being a woman of sense, she consoled instead of questioned until he was calm.

Later she gleaned from him a little—a very little—of what he had to tell. But for Miss Cartwright it was enough. Being a conscientious woman as well as a woman of sense, she interviewed his mother that same evening.

'Oliver is very imaginative,' she concluded. 'I don't think in his present state that Bitteme Hillside is good for him. I should not care to accept the responsibility. He is old enough now to go to a preparatory school.'

Next week Oliver left home for the first time to go to an establishment at Bournemouth, where he met other little boys, and was initiated into the mysteries of real cricket.

New and more vital interests entered Oliver's life and ousted the old. Back home for the holidays he still dreamed of Her, but not so often, nor did the formless impressions of the dreams remain with him so long. He still felt Her presence when he went to the summer-house alone, but not so acutely as before. He was losing touch with Her. As the age of innocence passed so did She pass with it.

He told nobody the whole story, although he was less diffident about it now, and would laugh with his mother about 'the time when I was frightened in the summer-house', and add, 'What a silly kid I must have been!'

Very little of the age of innocence survived his first two terms at Harrow, where he went after leaving the Bournemouth school. He had lost Her entirely now. He knew that he had lived in a world of imagination. He was puzzled, and a little troubled when he thought about it, but he did not often think. He lived now in a brisk, virile, noisy world, in which eccentricities, even of the mind, were not permissible.

At the age of nineteen he went up to Trinity College, Cambridge, and there, for the first time, discussed his early experiences with a friend. They were both of the opinion that 'kids were rummy little devils' whom no adult could ever properly understand.

Oliver never guessed there was to be a sequel. When it came it took him completely unawares.

It was in the long vacation after his second year at Cambridge. On a summer afternoon Oliver was lounging in flannels under the cedar tree on the lawn.

There was a tennis-court marked out now, and the net had been tightened for action. Beside Oliver was a tennis-racket in a press. His fingers screwed and unscrewed the swivels, and he kept asking himself impatiently why the devil Gladys always was so infernally late.

Gladys was the daughter of a neighbour, a girl in whom Oliver took a lukewarm interest. She came over to play tennis with him two or three afternoons a week. His mother, who had at last decided to be middle-aged, was resting. His father, now a bigger man than ever in the City, spent much of his time there, and only the week-ends saw him at Bitteme Hillside.

While Oliver was lamenting the unpunctuality of the fair Gladys, the butler—still the same Mr Beale, but older and stouter—opened the glass door which communicated with the hall, and set foot upon the garden-path.

Oliver sprang up.

'Is that Miss Baker?' he called.

Beale, after his fashion, vouchsafed no sign of having heard him, and did not speak until he had arrived at the conventional speaking distance.

'There is a gentleman to see you, Mr Oliver,' he said. 'Colonel Warlow.'

Oliver frowned over the name. It seemed vaguely familiar.

'Perhaps,' he suggested, 'he wants my father.'

'He asked for Mr Fowler. Shall I tell him'

'No,' said Oliver. 'I suppose I had better see him. Where is he? In the morning-room? Right!'

He found an upright old man, with a white moustache faintly tinged with yellow, standing by the window of the morning-room, and looking down the drive. The visitor glanced at Oliver in some mystification, and Oliver said, 'I expect you want my father, sir. I'm afraid he's away in town. Is there anything that I can do?'

The old man stared at him, and smiled.

'Of course,' he said, 'you must be Mr Fowler's son. I heard that there was a son, but I pictured you as a child. As one grows older one loses count of time. You've probably heard of me, Mr Fowler. I sold the house to your father many years ago.'

Oliver smiled broadly.

'Oh, yes!' he exclaimed. 'You've been abroad, haven't you, sir? It's jolly of you to come and call. The mater'

The old man interrupted courteously.

'Pray don't disturb her. I had a whim to come back and look at the old house and gardens. I returned to England last week after sixteen years. Perhaps, if you have five minutes to spare'

'I shall be delighted to' Oliver stopped short with a chuckle. 'I was going to say, "Show you round", but as you know the house much better than I do'

'You mean, accompany me. Thank you. The gardens must look charming now.'

'Would you like to see them? Or will you have some refreshment first?'

'A cup of tea presently, since you're so kind,' said the old man, 'but not just yet.'

Together they went to the glass door overlooking the rear of the house, and Colonel Warlow immediately began to exclaim, 'Ah, you've done away with two beds and lengthened that lawn over there. I thought of doing that myself. Tennis, I see. It used to be croquet in my day. The old cedar still looks fit enough. I heard cedars were dying all over England. I'm glad—'

It seemed to Oliver that the old man was fighting some emotion which he was afraid of becoming audible in his voice. He supposed it was poverty which had made him sell the place, and felt uncomfortable. He had no illusions about his origin, but he did not care to see himself as one of a race of monied interlopers.

Colonel Warlow's voice chimed in upon his thoughts.

'You were going to play tennis, I see. Please don't let me keep you.'

'No, no, sir. My opponent hasn't arrived yet. She's always about an hour late.'

Colonel Warlow smiled.

'It's good to know there are young people about here again. Tell me, have you knocked down the summer-house?'

'No, that still stands.' Oliver smiled reminiscently. 'It used to be a favourite spot of mine. Would you like to see it, sir?'

The old man led the way across the central lawn and through the shrubbery. Inside the summer-house he sat himself on the old worm-eaten bench.

'It's strange to be here again,' he said, in a muffled voice.

'People like to come back to places where they have been happy,' Oliver hazarded.

'A murderer cannot help returning to the scene of his crime.'

Oliver looked at the visitor in surprise: he had spoken so quietly and seriously.

'I killed my daughter, you know,' said Colonel Warlow. His voice thickened and he cleared his throat. 'It was through my fault. Haven't they told you that? I couldn't bear the house any longer without my Margery. Haven't they told you about it? If I hadn't been an obstinate old fool'

His voice thickened again, and died away.

'This was a favourite retreat of hers,' he continued, after a pause. 'She grew up. It's strange how a father scarcely realises when his daughter becomes a woman. Young men began to take a fancy to the house—you've heard about it all, perhaps?'

He spoke anxiously, as if fearful that Oliver would deny him the pleasure of tearing open his old wound. The young man shook his head, afraid lest his own voice might break the spell. He met the gaze of the old man's dim blue eyes and flinched before the sadness in them.

'Ah, well, it happened a long time ago! Little Margery was nineteen. There was one young fellow—it doesn't matter about his name—the people left here even before I did. Margery liked him, and I didn't. I'd nothing against him but my own dislike. I told them they were both too young. I suppose I didn't want to lose Margery. They—they used to meet in this summer-house. '

Oliver felt suddenly chilled, as if a cold draught had struck him. Old memories came back to him like a flock of birds on silent wings.

'I forbade any love-making,' the old man's dreary voice continued. 'I was used to seeing that my orders were obeyed. I found them here once and made a scene. I threatened to horsewhip him—poor fellow, he couldn't have lifted a hand against me. And do you know what I did? Do you know what I did, Mr Fowler?'

His shaken voice paused as if for a reply. There being none he continued, 'I drove them to meet clandestinely. I thought she'd given up seeing him. I didn't realise then that I was trying to give commands to Nature. They met elsewhere, and used to go up the river. I didn't know it until—oh, surely you know what happened now! He couldn't swim well enough to'

He broke off the thread of his speech once more, looked up, and nodded.

'Both of them!' he said.

Oliver was staring out through the trellis-work window at the foliage beyond.

Those strange experiences of childhood—were they, after all, imaginary? Or had there lingered about the place some woman-spirit who loved children and had made her presence real to a lonely little boy? It was never her fault when he had felt afraid

'Used she to wear a dress of peacock blue?'

It was Oliver who spoke, although he scarcely recognized his own voice.

'That was the dress she was drowned in, sir. Somebody must have told you'

There followed another spell of silence, which was broken at last by a girl's voice from the lawn.

'Oliver! Ol-i-ver!'

Miss Baker had arrived, had been shown out into the garden, and was now making her presence known. Colonel Warlow's features relaxed into the ghost of a smile.

'I think somebody wants you to play tennis,' he said. 'Please do. If you will allow me, I will sit here alone for a little while.'

Wrastler's End

You turn east from St Fay Harbour and take the cliff path which leads you, after a mile of scrambling, to Relland Cove, you must climb two precipitous hills. The second is the higher and the steeper, but the climber is rewarded for his labours, for on reaching the pinnacle he is given such a view of Relland as only a bird might enjoy if no hill were there to be climbed.

He will see the half-dozen farmhouses and scattered cottages which are all that is left of habitations in Relland parish today, old Relland Church embowered in trees and looking like a little grey bird in a nest, the gracious rise and fall of the long fields, the curve of the bay where blue water meets yellow sand in a thin line of foam, and the towering cliff beyond, whose rugged face is relieved from sternness by pink and roseate tints showing here and there on the surface of the rocks. The headland whence this picture of Relland may be seen is called Wrastler's End.

Most visitors to a strange place take local names for granted unless such names be so quaint or incongruous as to court enquiry into their origin. A thousand strangers climb to Wrastler's End and go their ways unwondering, to one who troubles to speculate how the peak of a cliff had come by such a name. It happened that I was of an enquiring turn of mind, and fell to speculating on what the name could mean: for Wrastler's End is the end of nothing at all. The cliff path continues to wander, dropping downwards to sea-level and reappears again at the far edge of Relland sands.

It was some minutes before it occurred to me that in Cornwall a wrestler is called a 'wrastler', and then I guessed easily enough that at some time in the past a local champion had met his death in that vicinity.

No effort of deduction was needed to take one a further step. Rusty railings flank the path thereabouts on the seaward side. Before those railings were set, there was likely enough no barrier to save one from falling from that dizzy height on to the rocks sheer below. A slip of the foot on a dark night, and the thing was done.

Having, as I thought, solved a little problem of etymology, I continued my way and thought of other things. An hour later, after I had seen over Relland Church, I was idly looking about the graveyard when I came to a stone sacred to the memory of Abraham Tuckey, 'who met his death at the righteous hands of Enoch Holten on the eighth of February, 1814.'

Underneath was an epitaph in the form of verses, but these were unintelligible, for the lower part of the stone had become already the prey of moss and lichen. Probably the upper half had at some time been scoured by somebody who did not think it worthwhile to preserve the doggerel underneath. But I could still pick out a word or two here and there, and occasionally the full half of a line. And one of these lines ended with the words, 'his wrestling done'.

Now here, thought I, was likely enough the grave of the man who had given Wrastler's End its peculiar name; and then my attention wandered back to the upper half of the stone. I liked the reference to the 'righteous hands' of Enoch Holten. One sees almost incredible things on tombstones in remote Cornish villages, where at one time all manner of queer codes of morals were subscribed to by a mysterious and lawless people. This might well be red murder, condoned by the neighbourhood and thus unblushingly left on record. Those were the days of smugglers, and that coast was notorious for its free-trading.

Idly, I began to weave a story. This Enoch Holten was a smuggler whom Abraham Tuckey had betrayed to the excise officers, and one night afterwards the two men had met face to face up there on the peak of the cliff, and Tuckey had gone to his death over the lip of rock where now the railings stood. Yes, but this Tuckey had been a wrestler.

Here was I on the scent of a mystery, and I fell to wondering if it were too late, after a hundred years, to learn the truth of it. I was in a land of old stories, traditions, and long memories. Doubtless there were those about St Fay who could tell me the whole story of the affair at which the tombstone thus teasingly hinted, but I had not learned to make this secretive people talk. They hoard their stores of old songs and legends, but they have little or nothing to tell strangers.

If my curiosity were already aroused, it was deeply intrigued before I left the churchyard; for, having turned from the grave of Abraham Tuckey I found the grave of Enoch Holten. Here there was no epitaph, nor any inscription beyond the man's name and the date of his death. According to that which was written on the stone, he had passed away on the twenty-fourth of December, 1813. I am not too quick-witted, and it was after some moments that I became aware of the discrepancy. One stone alleged that Enoch Holten had killed Abraham Tuckey, and, according to the other, Enoch Holten had died first by a margin of some weeks.

Obviously, it seemed to me, there had either been a mistake on the part of the mason, or there were two Enoch Holtens. Holten was still a common name in St Fay, and there was still a disposition to go to the Old Testament for 'Christian' names. It was not unlikely that there were two contemporary Enoch Holtens, and this gave wider possibilities to the story I had begun to trace.

At once I drew a bow at a venture and winged an idea. These two Enoch Holtens were close kinsmen. When one died the other blamed Abraham Tuckey for his death, and took vengeance into his own hands. I looked in vain for the grave of the second Enoch Holten, and surmised that, if the first stone were truthfully inscribed, he had probably been hanged at Bodmin Gaol.

As a writer and a reader I have always loved a mystery for its own sake, and here, I was sure, was a story of more than ordinary interest if only the record of it remained and could be unearthed. So on my return to St Fay I bought a 'history' of the place, written by a local gentleman who, embarrassed by the honour of being printed, had written in the stilted and flowery language of one earnestly intent on keeping his literary style on its best behaviour.

As a guide-book it was quite a success, but as a history it was curiously incomplete. There were many references to the past, but these were mostly vague generalities. Beauty spots were mentioned and described abundantly, and the works of nature were praised with a hint or two of patronage.

Wrastler's End was referred to as a noble headland, but no hint was given as to the origin of its name. The architectural beauties of Relland Church were described, but nothing was said about those two graves. Finding the book useless, I flung it down in disgust and determined to hear the story in St Fay by word of mouth.

It was easier determined than done. I set about my task by making frank enquiries of the older men who came of an evening to the Sailor's Rest for pipe and pint. They were friendly and civil, but none had anything to tell me. They said that they did not know, and had changed the subject as quickly as they could. One or two of the more communicative admitted that they'd 'heered as Wrastler's End got its name through a wrastler gettin' killed thereabouts', but they knew no more than that. Nor could any enlighten me concerning the two graves in Relland churchyard, with the strange inscription on the one and the contradictory date on the other.

I took to spending part of every evening in the Sailors' Rest, and was soon on terms of cordiality with most of the customers. For the most part they were good fellows who only wanted knowing, glad of an excuse for laughing, and, like most of their kind, responsive enough to tact diluted with a little beer. Nearly all had been born and bred in the village, and worked in the boats or on the land. Jerry Plint, the landlord, was himself a native, but he had seen more of the world than the others, having served his full time in the Navy. He was a sprightly veteran of seventy who might have passed for fifty, and he took a liking to me and seemed glad to see me on his settle. Indeed, I flattered myself that I was popular in the village.

For a time I thought the story I was in search of had been irretrievably lost. Then something —some kind of sixth sense—told me otherwise. They all knew it and wouldn't tell me. They had heard it from their fathers and mothers, who had heard it from folk who were alive at the time when that happened at Wrastler's End which earned the place its name. As they grew to know me better, I could tell from chance words dropped when I tried to re-open the subject—the least hint from one man and frowns from all the others—that they had the whole story at their finger-tips. But if they liked me well enough, I was still a stranger and a 'foreigner', and it was not to be shared with me. They were like children, hoarding some useless secret.

Curiosity and obstinacy made me swear to learn it, but I was still baulked of my object when my stay came to an end. But I returned several times for a week or a fortnight at a stretch, for I liked St Fay and the place suited me. And it took me nearly three years to learn the story of Wrastler's End.

I don't suppose I should ever have learned it, but for the fact of old Jerry Plint having got himself involved in some mild litigation with one of the local bigwigs, from which my knowledge of the law—I had once practised as a solicitor—was able to extract him scathless. Jerry was grateful, but his gratitude took no tangible shape for a little while. Generally the Sailors' Rest was well patronized of an evening, but sometimes when the fishing-boats were out, and there was some local entertainment to lure the others from beer and gossip, old Jerry was wont to say that he 'might just so well put up shutters'.

On such an evening in February I entered the bar and found myself alone on the public side of the counter, and old Jerry leaning on the other side of it, staring disconsolately at a fire which bade fair to bum all his evening's profits. He drank with me, and we stood with the counter between us talking.

"Tis a whist drive up to the schools,' said Jerry, nodding at the empty settles, 'and the boats out over to the Lizard. 'Tis a fine night surely. I reckon usil have good weather now until the change of the moon.'

He paused to fill a short clay pipe with black shag.

'The winters hereabouts keep just so fine as the summers,' he continued. 'I reckon it was just such a night as this—no moon, but a brave show of stars—that my grandfather saw Wrastler Tuckey thrown. 'Twas the first time he was ever thrown, and the last, and then it wasn't mortal man as threw him. Sheer he went from the top of Wrastler's End, and took with him a yard of oak fence which was splintered like matches.'

I looked up quickly to see a meaning and humorous light in Jerry's old, sea-blue eyes.

'Ah!' I exclaimed softly.

'You've been asking for the story off and on for years,' he continued, 'but none 'ud tell 'ee. They're queer people here, sir. I don't rightly know why they kep' quiet. Maybe they didn't want a gentleman from London to think they was liars, or else fools, for believing what my grandfather knew was gospel. I've often been minded to tell 'ee, but them others, they wouldn't like it if they knew. So you won't let on that I've told 'ee.

'And you couldn't hear it from a better man, for I heered it from my grandfather's own lips when I was a boy. 'Twas he that saw the miracle happen, and came nigh being hung for it. You'll not believe the tale, but my grandfather, sir, he'd got religion along with the Wesleyans, and if he'd once known how to tell a lie he'd forgotten long before I was born. He was over eighty when he died back in 'seventy-six; one of them small, spare men that never seem to wear out. I mind him as if I'd only seed him yesterday.'

I smiled in anticipation of having my curiosity quenched at last.

'Was your grandfather Enoch Holten?' I asked.

'God forbid!' he answered simply. 'But I'll tell 'ee the whole story, if you're minded to listen and not let on that I've told 'ee. Besides, sir, you've seen this Enoch Holten's grave.'

'I though there must have been two of that name,' said I. 'Either that, or they made a mistake with the date on his stone.'

Jerry shook his head slowly.

'There weren't no mistake. Enoch died before Abraham Tuckey. That's the queer part o' the story. I told 'ee that it was no mortal man as killed Abraham Tuckey.'

And here follows Jerry Plint's story, told in his own words so far as I am able to recall them.

'This Enoch Holten was a quarryman and he lived a mile up the hill in that old cottage which stands beside the pit to this day. In the year eighteen-thirteen he'd have been about twenty-eight, and a fine strapping fellow, from my grandfather's account. He was a steady, serious sort o' chap, and the best wrastler we had then along this stretch o' coast.

"Twas all wrastlin' in them days. Down here they never took much count o' the prize ring. Wrastlin's come back a bit, but 'tesn't what it was. In them days they talked wrastlin', dreamed of wrastlin', and lived for wrastlin', just like they do of football today. So you may lay to it that Enoch was a popular man, and, being good-looking into the bargain, he could have had his picking of the maids about here, so 'twasn't much to wonder at that he should take up sweethearting with Mary Penrowan, who was comelier than all the others put together. My grandfather, sir, he had a fancy for Mary, but his chance looked gone when Enoch took to walking over to Relland of an evening. For my grandfather was a shrimp of a man, and nothing to look at, who made his living by a bit o' fishing and a bit o' free trading.

'In them days there was a heap of smuggling done in these parts, and King George the Third didn't seem able to stop it no how, in spite of the excise officers and the soldiers, who were always causing trouble. I reckon Enoch may have had a finger in that pie, too, for landsmen as well as seamen took a hand in the game. However, smugglin' don't come into the story, except that if my old grandfather hadn't been on the lookout that night for the Fowey Queen, which was expected home from one of the French ports with a cargo o' contraband—But I mustn't go telling the story tail-end first.

'It must have been in the summer of 'thirteen that Enoch Holten met more than his match at the wrastlin' over to Bodmin. 'Twas a youngster from over to Polruan, a dark horse, as the sayin' is, who robbed Enoch of the belt, to the disappointment of nearly every man, woman, and child in these parts. There wasn't anything on wheels left in St Fay and Relland that day, for every horse and cart had taken its load to Bodmin, and lots more had gone on foot. Mary Penrowan was there, as a matter o' course, and see her man beaten for the first time.

"Twas a fair bout, from all accounts, and even the folks from St Fay couldn't say different; but Enoch Holten took a bad toss, and when it came to his leavin' the ring he had to be carried. This Abraham Tuckey, who had bested him, was a chap of five-and-twenty, who'd been trainin' in secret along of an old champion. Likely enough there was money won and lost on that bout. Physically, he was just about so proper a man as Enoch, but he was different in all else, for Enoch was a fair man and Abraham Tuckey was as dark as a Spaniard, with black flashing eyes which scared most men and drew most women like as if they were moths. Them eyes of his he flashed on Mary Penrowan when he was all flushed with victory, and Mary stood by the ringside half crying because her man was beaten and all in a flutter of worry because he was hurt. My grandfather reckoned the mischief began then and there, for after that Mary Penrowan couldn't keep her thoughts oil him, and although she went home hating him, 'tes the way love starts with some sorts o' women.

'Well, sir, they soon found out as Enoch Holten had come to worse grief than was at first supposed. The fall had done something to his back, and he lay for weeks afterwards in bed.

When he got up at last he walked like an old man, and his body was shrunken, and 'twas easy to see that even if he got better he'd never be his old self again. I reckon Mary would have stuck to him and married him and lived and died a happy woman if Abraham Tuckey hadn't come to St Fay. There's no doubt she was the bait as brought him here. He'd a bit o' money, and he left Polruan and bought a share in a St Fay boat. Maybe he wouldn't have been so welcome here, but the people had lost their champion, and were, maybe, minded to have another, even if he wasn't a proper St Fay man. Besides, there was none as dared to say much to Abraham Tuckey.

'Nobody liked him much at first, and nobody never did like him much, and there was rare talk when he set those eyes of his on Mary Penrowan for the second time. Like a needle he drew her with those eyes of his for a magnet, and she came to him just so helpless as a bird caught by the looks of a snake. I reckon he was bad through and through. Most people blamed the girl, but my grandfather always said as she couldn't help herself.

'Everybody could see the way things were moving before 'twas admitted by Mary herself that Enoch was not to be her man after all, and it was common property whom she meant to marry long before a public word was said to her or Abraham Tuckey. The new champion took to walking over to Relland whenever his boat was in, and Mary was seen walking with him of evenings just as she had used to walk with Enoch Holten.

'As for Enoch, nobody never knew exactly what he thought of it all, for he grew queer and silent as the fires in him burnt low. He'd lost the championship and his health and the girl he loved, and all the sweetness of life must have turned sour in the man's mouth.

'Everybody was sorry for him, but nobody said much to him, for it didn't seem fitty-like to remind him of his sorrows. And as he shut himself up and was seldom seen abroad, it wasn't so strange that Abraham Tuckey had been living in the parish for some weeks before the two met face to face.

'That happened here in the village, close to where the post-office stands today. Mary was on Abraham Tuckey's arm, and one or two of the women standing about—for 'twas a fine evening—made a noise like geese to show the couple, especially Mary, what they thought of 'em.

'Abraham Tuckey deigned to take no notice, but wore his head high, and when they came face to face with Enoch Holten, walkin' slow and leanin' on his stick, he stopped dead, although Mary would have pulled him by.

' "Enoch Holten," says Abraham Tuckey, "there's people here thinkin' ill things of me and Mary, and sayin' ill things behind my back. And I ask 'ee so all can hear, and expect an answer so as all can here—did I throw 'ee fair or foul, Enoch Holten?"

'And Enoch spoke up in answer, though not so loud, for his voice was weaker.

' "Fair enough for a dirty thief!" says he.

'He was looking at Mary as he spoke, and then he spat upon the ground.

'Abraham took another step towards him, with Mary dragging at his arm

' "'Tes lucky for you, Enoch Holten, that you be a broken man," says he

' "'Tes lucky for one of us I be a broken man. But I bean't so broken I can't be mended, Abraham Tuckey, and I'll throw 'ee yet, as God's my witness. The dead shall rise before ever 'ee take Mary Penrowan to church with 'ee."

'Them that was listenin' admired the man's spirit, and Abraham Tuckey must have felt which way the sympathy was going, although none uttered a word.

' "'Tes easy threatenin'," says he with a laugh. "You with both your feet in the grave."

' "Livin' or dead," says Enoch Holten, "I'll throw 'ee yet!"

'But the man's spirit was stronger than his body, and come the fall of the year 'twas easy seen he wasn't long for this world. It must have been Christmas Eve or thereabouts when his body was found washing in a foot of surf in Relland Bay. How he got into the sea, and if 'twere suicide or not, none knew, and crowner's jury brought in a verdict of "Death by misadventure", so as not to keep the poor body out of holy ground.

'Not long after Christmas the banns of Abraham Tuckey and Mary Penrowan was read out in church. I know by the date on Abraham's stone that they was to have been married on the ninth of February, because the queerest part of this story happened on the eighth.

'That night Abraham Tuckey called for Mary over to Relland, and they went for their last walk together as lover and maid before becoming, as they thought, man and wife. The rest my grandfather told me with his own lips, and you may believe or not, sir, as you're minded.

'That was before my grandfather got salvation along with the Wesleyans, sir, and he had a share in a free trader called the Fowey Queen, which was expected to lie off that very night and wait for the signal of a clear coast.

'The best place to watch was from the top of the cliff which was afterwards called Wrastler's End, but 't wasn't safe, for the Customs men would have pounced like tigers on anyone showing a light there.

'So my grandfather, sir, he climbed to the tower of Relland Church, which was almost so good. Directly he got his answering signal from the sea, 'twould be seen all down the coast, and there was some to light a Hare six miles to the east, and to set the hunt galloping in that direction.

'It was a clear night without a moon, but too many stars for my grandfather's liking. He sat there fidgeting and waiting and got no sign from the sea. It so chanced that the Fowey

Queen was delayed two days, which was just so well; for there was such a to-do in the place by that time that she ran in and landed her cargo without a shot being fired.

'After a while, sir, my grandfather got tired of watching the sea, and cast his eyes downward at the graveyard far below him. He looked idly-like at first, and then he stared, for he seed something moving. In the darkness he could just make out Enoch Holten's grave, for 'twas the newest there, and made a pale-looking patch on the ground, by reason that the grass hadn't yet grown on it. It looked to him, he said, just so as if somebody was rising up out of that grave, so that his heart thumped with fear and he started thinkin' of the Day o' Judgment.

'But my grandfather, not being a religious man in them days, didn't rightly believe in the Resurrection; or, if he did, he remembered as he was a free trader, and business was business, and he didn't like people in the churchyard while he was engaged up in the tower 'pon private matters. My grandfather couldn't see too clearly, but clear enough to make sure that 'twas only one man he had to deal with; and for one man he cared little, him having his pistols with him. He cocked them then and there, which wasn't too wise, him having them narrow worn stone stairs to go down. You could take a fall on them as easy then as you can today, but my grandfather, although he hurried, got down 'em all right without breaking his neck or shooting himself.

'He passed out through the little door and went on tiptoe round to the front facing the sea. And as he walked, someone came to meet him, stepping swiftly over the graves. Before my grandfather could utter a word he saw who 'twas; and a great fear came on him so that he fell on his knees and covered his eyes with his hands.

'For 'twas Enoch Holten, who'd been dead nearly seven weeks, that came to meet him. There was no mistaking his face, although now it had turned the colour of mud. Although he was a landsman he had always worn a fisherman's blue jersey and a red stocking cap, and so they had buried him, and so he now stood before my grandfather.

'Neither spoke for a time, which seemed an age to my grandfather, in fact, not until he made shift to start praying, and then Enoch Holten cut him off sharp and stem—which made my grandfather sure that Enoch had come back from the bad place.

' "Amos Plint," says Enoch Holten solemnly—for that was my grandfather's name—"stand up and follow me, and bear witness if I throw him fair. For I am come back to keep my vow and you shall speak for me before the world."

'With that my grandfather felt himself powerless but to do as he was bid. So shaken was he that afterwards, when he came to think of it, he marvelled at being able to stand, let alone walk.

'And then the man that had come back out of the grave turned right about, and walked before him to the gate of the churchyard. He opened it and passed through, my grandfather following a yard or two behind. From what he said he had no more option but to follow than if he'd been a cart behind a horse.

'He was dazed-like, and yet he noticed things. Enoch Holten seemed as real and solid as you and me. His steps made no sound 'pon the road, but as they climbed the cliff path my grandfather heard him breathing heavy like a live thing, and the small loose stone spurting from under his feet.

'As they drew towards the peak of the cliff my grandfather turned his eyes upwards and saw the headland sheer against the sky with nothing moving on the top. Only before him he saw Enoch Holten toiling upwards, like a black blot in the shape of a man. My grandfather was feared that something dreadful was to happen, but he grew more hopeful as they came nigh the top. He said as he counted more and more stars coming into sight at every step, and breathed the easier for seeing nothing moving on the skyline.

'You know the top of Wrastler's End? From both sides 'tes a steep climb, and there's maybe twenty yards of level path on top. In them days there was no iron railings, but there was a bit of oak fence in the place where the railings now stand. My grandfather guessed that Enoch Holten had come to meet Abraham Tuckey, and when at last they reached the top and saw no one I reckon he uttered a prayer of thankfulness.

'But if he did he spoke too soon, for he'd hardly got his breath before he heard voices, and saw the head and shoulders of Abraham Tuckey and Mary Penrowan. They were climbing the hill from the other side and their gaze was bent downwards, so as they didn't see nothing at first. My grandfather tried to cry out to them, but found his tongue locked fast behind his teeth.

They were on their way back to Mary's home, and their arms were wound about each other's waists.

'Enoch Holten stood in the middle of the path, and as they drew nigh he dropped into the posture of a wrastler. And at that moment Tuckey, having reached the summit, saw him and stood suddenly still.

'Never a word was uttered, and that seemed to my grandfather as queer as anything else. He heard a scream from the maid, and a laugh from Abraham Tuckey. 'Twas the laugh of a man who knows his last hour is come and yet won't show fear. And that was all.

'Tuckey shook himself free of Mary Penrowan and stepped up like a man to meet his doom. He, too, fell into the attitude of a wrastler, and the two of them met and held and swayed. For a full minute, my grandfather reckoned, they swayed on the edge of the path, and all the time they were so silent as shadows thrown by moonlight against a wall.

'And then it seemed as if Abraham Tuckey was gathered up like a child and pushed against the oak fence. And it gave way as easy as rotted wreck-wood, but with the sound of a gunshot, and the two figures vanished. Not a cry he heard, but one or two faint thuds like something falling from ledge to ledge, and after that there was silence. There was only my grandfather there and Mary Penrowan, facing each other wild-eyed in the gloom.

'How he got Mary home that night, and how he got himself home, my grandfather doesn't rightly remember. Luckily for him, my grandfather thought it best to tell the whole truth to magistrate and parson; else I dare say they might have hanged him. Even as it was the magistrate had his doubts, but when he and Mary was examined separately and told the same story the magistrate began to scratch his head. You see 'twould have been impossible for a man like my grandfather to have thrown Abraham Tuckey, even with Mary to help him. I don't reckon five ordinary men of my grandfather's build could have done it, let be that a strong oak fence had splintered like match-sticks.

'There was only one body found, Abraham Tuckey's. In one of his hands was found a piece of blue woollen stuff which might have been tom from a jersey, only t'was as rotten as a medlar.

'So the justices, when they met, agreed as there was no evidence, especially as he could have shot Abraham Tuckey if he'd been minded to murder him; and 'twas against nature to suppose he could have thrown him.

'It made a stir in these parts as was never forgotten by them as lived through it. People reckoned as Enoch Holten had been allowed to come back as a minister of vengeance from heaven; but my grandfather, he reckoned as heaven hadn't got much to do with that business, and being a scared man from that hour forward he went and got religion.

'As time wore on there was people who didn't know anything about it said that this here Tuckey had been set upon and murdered by free traders because they suspected him of spying. I dare say 'twas my grandfather marrying Mary Penrowan as started that tale.

'Oh, yes, didn't I tell 'ee, sir, as he married her after all? Mary Plint she became, and Mary Plint's name you'll find in Relland churchyard if you go to look. My own father was her second boy. But she died 'fore I was born, so I never seed more'n an old picture of her.'

The Gamblers' Room

Within a minute of the numbers going up after the last race the enclosures of Kempton Park began to disgorge their crowds. Broad streams of humanity flowed sluggishly through the exits, to be broken up outside, the main currents streaming towards the station, while tributaries moved in the direction where the cars were parked and where assorted vehicles waited to convey chance passengers to the tramlines at Hampton.

I was in no hurry. Dusk was already falling—the early dusk of winter—but the evening was young. I decided that I would have tea somewhere quietly and catch a later train when the mob was gone. A few steps take one over the railway bridge into Sunbury, which is still more a village than a suburb. I found it as quiet as if it were Sunday afternoon, and had tea alone in the back of a little baker's shop on the Staines Road.

I must have sat long over tea, reading the evening paper, for it was dark when I came out, and the pubs were open. My head still ached a little from the bustle and roar of Tattersalls' earlier in the day, and when it occurred to me that a whisky-and-soda might put it right I took the necessary steps.

There was a fair crowd in the bar, and I could tell from the looks of them that a nucleus of racegoers had decided like myself to linger a little in the neighbourhood. While I stood waiting to be served I found myself overhearing scraps of talk from two men standing at my elbow, and I understood from the chance fragments of speech wafted in my direction that they were old acquaintances who had met there accidentally after some considerable lapse of time.

They were a strangely assorted pair. One man was admirably dressed and might have stood for a model of unobtrusive smartness. It was easy to hazard where he had been, for a case of binoculars depending from a shoulder-strap hung over his hips. He was standing with his back to me, but when he moved his head I had occasional glimpses of his profile. I judged him at once to be a man of about my own age, a good-looking fellow with a slightly aquiline cast of features and that indefinable air of well-being which springs from perfect health and a lack of financial anxieties.

His companion looked a little older and was his antithesis in every way.

From the top of his shabby hat to the worn uppers of his boots he looked the complete racecourse tout. He was seedy and unclean, his eyes restless and bloodshot, and he certainly had not shaved during the past forty-eight hours. Only the man spoke like a gentleman and the two were conversing in tones of easy familiarity.

I was looking at this unsavoury specimen when suddenly he raised his eyes to meet mine. I had no desire to be caught looking at him inquisitively, nor to indulge in a staring-out competition, so I turned my head. But at the same moment I heard an exclamation from him, and he pushed past his companion to confront me.

'Well, of all the—the last man I ever expected to see again! Isn't it Gedge?'

Gedge happens to be my name, but I could only stare at him blankly.

'You don't know me,' he continued, and added, with a deprecatory laugh, 'Well, I daresay I've changed more than you have. I should have known you anywhere. Don't you remember me at school—Paston?' It was nearly twenty years ago, but the moment after he had spoken I could see the boy he was in the man who now stood before me. Only the man was a gross caricature of the boy, so that amazement got the better of good manners and I could do no more than stare at him in surprise and dismay. You see, I remembered Paston the boy so vividly. He had been so very much the perfect youth that most of us respected him far more than we liked him. He was what we called "pi", a neat, quiet, fastidious, clever fellow, who showed in his teens, marked signs of the ascetic; and a boy cannot be an ascetic without being a prig. He was just the type which a housemaster marks down as a future prefect during his very first term, and when I had last seen him at eighteen or nineteen I should have said that he was the last sort of fellow to whom the grosser vices would offer any temptations. That Paston had become the thing I saw before me was something more than horrible—it was uncanny.

He uttered an ugly, hard, careless laugh as if he read my thoughts.

'It's most extraordinary!' he continued. 'First of all I ran into Storman, whom I hadn't seen for years, and within about two minutes you came breezing in. Do you know each other? Storman—Gedge.'

Storman and I exchanged doubtful nods. We were both quite reasonably a little suspicious of Paston's friends.

'I didn't see you at the races,' I said to Paston, filling an awkward pause.

'I suppose you were there?'

'Oh, you wouldn't have seen me. I was in the six-bob ring. Things haven't been going too well lately. I say, I want to have a yarn with you most awfully. You're not in a hurry, are you? Don't run away. I've got to go, but I'll be back in less than half an hour.'

I looked doubtfully at the clock and met the doubtful gaze of Storman. We had both an excuse to go, but curiosity had set a grip on us.

'Look here,' Paston continued, sinking his voice to an excited whisper.

'It's like this. Foyster's head lad is a pal of mine, and he's promised to meet me and let me know if they've got anything spinning tomorrow. I must go and see him. If you'll hang on for a bit we can have a yarn, and I'll tell you if that stable's got anything good.'

And this was Paston. Great heavens!

Although we made no promise he left us with an air of assurance that he would find us there on his return. The door swung behind him, leaving Storman and I standing elbow to elbow, a little conscious of our own respectability, and not knowing what in the world to say to each other.

'I suppose I shall wait,' I said at last.

'I suppose I shall, too,' Storman said.

Behind the speech of both of us was the unspoken thought that it would be rather cruel to go away before Paston returned. And although neither would have dreamed of saying it we knew that we were going to be 'touched'.

'Extraordinary meeting Paston here,' I blundered on.

'Extraordinary. I say, you going to have a drink?'

He gave an order. More silence followed.

'You know Paston well?' Storman asked presently in his suave conversational tone.

'No.' I hated to think that I heard a faint defensive ring in my own voice.

'I knew him at school, but I haven't seen him since.'

'Ah! I was with him at Cambridge. We came up the same term and kept on the same staircase at Corpus. We were friends.'

This cleared the air a little, but once more we found ourselves with nothing to say. Each of us was conscious that it would hardly be good form to discuss poor old Paston. But the change in the man seemed to beg comment from us both. It loomed up before us too monstrous to be ignored.

It was like trying to ignore a mountain or an earthquake.

'What was he like up at the 'Varsity?' I asked presently. I wondered when the change in Paston had begun to take place, and I was angling for information.

'Pretty much as he was at school, I dare say,' Storman replied.

'I remember in his last term,' I said with a reminiscent smile, 'he put a stop to the Sixth Form Derby Sweep. He was head boy then, and he threatened to call a prefects' meeting and raise Cain.'

'He never touched a horse or a card all the time he was at Cambridge. He was a good deal too quiet for me; not that I was a blood or anything like that. But he gave me the sort of companionship I sometimes wanted, and we spent a good part of the vacs together. Clever chap he was. Took a First in History, I remember.'

'Ah!' I said. 'Then you don't know any more than I do.'

'About what?'

'About Paston. The change in him. I don't want to run the poor devil down, but you must see it for yourself. It's impossible to ignore it. I can't think what can have brought him to his present pass. I remember having a vague impression at school that his people had plenty of money.'

'Oh, Paston came into more money than most of us will ever see. But he soon went through it. When a fellow starts betting in thousands'

'But he was the last fellow to bet even in shillings.'

'He was until—something happened.'

There was another pause. Storman, as I had suspected, evidently knew more than I.

'I like going to race meetings,' I remarked, 'and I enjoy having an occasional little flutter, but I'm dashed if I'd ruin myself for the benefit of the bookies. And it's such a queer bug for Paston of all people to be bitten by.'

Storman nodded.

'If you knew how it started,' he said, 'you wouldn't blame the poor devil. That's if you believed the facts.'

'How?' I began.

'I've just been turning over in my mind whether I ought to tell you or not,' he continued. 'It's only fair to Paston, but I doubt if it'll be fair to me. You'll be much too polite to hint that I'm lying, but I don't see how I can reasonably expect you not to think it. And if you don't think that you'll think I dreamed it all. And I didn't. The more I think of it the more sure I am that the ghastly thing really happened. It's the only way to account for the Paston we've just met today.'

'I should like to hear,' I murmured.

'Well, then, I'll tell you. It's only fair to Paston. And you can think what you like. . . . Let's go and sit in the comer over there where it's quiet. I dare say I shall have time to tell you before Paston comes back. I don't suppose it's necessary to warn you, but—please not a word to him. He doesn't know a thing about it and I don't suppose it 'ud do him any good if he did.'

All this was very mysterious and more than enough to pique my curiosity. I followed Storman into a quiet and dark comer of the room and we sat down cheek by jowl on the same side of a little table, while he told me the following extraordinary story.

'I've told you,' Storman began, 'that I met Paston first at Cambridge when we were both in our first term. Like me he'd come up straight from school with only the long vacation in between, so I suppose I must have started knowing him where you left off.

'I didn't like him very much at first. Having known him pretty well at school you'll understand why. He was the intellectual, highly superior, touch-me-not sort, and put on the airs of a junior don from his first day in College. If it hadn't been for a certain number of fellows from your old school who came up with him, and seemed able to stand him, he'd have been pretty badly barred at first. Not that he ever said or did anything offensive; it was just that frigid, pitying, condescending way of his.

'For some reason or reasons unknown he rather took to me—it was queer, because I wasn't his sort—and I was suddenly surprised to find myself rather liking the fellow. That was the first step to getting to know a bit about him. And the more I learned the more I liked.

'Paston was just as harmless and decent as they make 'em. He was just a serious-minded fellow, and he hadn't got an ounce of real side. What we thought was side was just a manner he was born with, and he could no more help it than he could help his face. He wasn't what you would call "pi", either, in the real sense of the word. Drinking, gambling, and discreditable love affairs simply had no attractions for him. Directly I really grasped his point of view I could understand and rather envy him. He was what in those days we should have called a "trout".

' "My dear fellow," he said to me once, when I tried to rope him into a poker party, "it would simply bore me to tears. I don't say that I never play cards. When I'm at home I occasionally have to make up a four at bridge, but I'd sooner do anything else. I've got a certain amount of money to spare and I don't want to take money away from some other man who may want every penny he's got. Nor would it give me any pleasure to lose. Nobody can say that gambling is a good thing. All that can be urged for it is that in certain circumstances it may not be very harmful. Why, then, should I dabble with a vice which doesn't attract me in the least?"

'Yes, he said that—he, who within seven or eight years from that day put something like a hundred and fifty thousand pounds into the pockets of bookmakers and tipsters.

'I must have led a sort of double life at the 'Varsity. I mixed with a pretty lively set, but when I got tired of it—which I often did—I liked going to Paston for a serious jaw. Together we discussed the riddle of the Universe, the hereafter, religion, and every other thing, after the manner of boys of twenty. Paston, I found, was in a very enviable position. His father was a rich man—something to do with the wine trade, I believe. But he already had property in trust for him, against the time of his coming of age, left him by his maternal grandfather. It looked as if he'd never have to do a stroke of work, but he didn't enjoy the prospect for its own sake.

'What he was going to do with his life was a problem to which he couldn't find an answer. He wanted to have work, and to do something useful. His religious convictions weren't orthodox enough for him to contemplate entering the Church. He had no use for politics, or, rather he had no use for professional politicians. The Bar was overcrowded, and even if he were able to make good he would only be taking bread out of the mouths of other good men who needed it. When I suggested once that the Senior Common-room was the ideal place for him he laughed and said that even in the very unlikely event of his name coming up for election, that semi-monastic life hardly fitted in with his ideas of being useful to the community.

'When I had had pretty broad hints both from home and from my college tutor that it was time I settled down to work, I saw more and more of Paston. He worked tolerably hard himself, and it was easy to work in his company. His tripos was the same as mine and he was able to help me more than a little. It was all through him that I managed to scrape a second. That's how we started paying each other visits during the vacs, and sometimes went off together on walking or cycling tours. Paston's father and mother were awfully nice, and it was partly for their sake that I afterwards sweated blood in trying to get rid of the devil that came to possess poor old Paston. But it wasn't any good, as you can see. I was only human, and something more than human had got a stranglehold on him. You'll understand what I mean by that presently.

'It was in our last year that the thing happened. It must have been about Boat Race time, and it was in the spring vacation just prior to our last term. That's a restless time of the year for men just rising twenty-two. Even now I'm getting forty-ish I get recurrences of the old spring fret, you know, and want to take the stiffness out of my limbs on footpaths and strange roads. We'd both got it badly then, a wanderlust bred by the divine discontent of youth, a sort of itch to go somewhere and find that beautiful, mysterious, and dangerous young woman whose name is Adventure.

'It ended in our slinging some books and a change or two of linen into a couple of rucksacks and starting out for a week or two. We didn't know where we were going. We made no plans. We were just going to see the pageant of an English spring, and spend our nights wherever chance happened to take us. Only once did we plan to visit any particular place, and that was when Paston, studying the map one evening, announced that Great Chowney was only about thirty miles away.

' "Let's walk over there tomorrow," he suggested. "I've got a place there I'd rather like you to see. One of the bits of property my grandfather left me. It's quite small—he used to use it as a hunting-box—but it's awfully jolly. When I'm an old man and want somewhere to end my days in peace I think I shall settle down there and grow roses."

'From what he told me it was a perfect specimen of one of those little Jacobean manor houses, with a bit of garden, an orchard, and a paddock—the sort of place which fetches about £3,000 in the market and gets advertised in the big illustrated weeklies. I should say that this description was just about adequate, but I never saw right over the place. Well, we made for Great Chowney on the following day, and I wish to Heaven we hadn't.

'Paston explained that the house was empty, so that we couldn't sleep there, but added that there was a good inn at the place. We arrived as tired as dogs, just as dusk was falling, to find the village packed to suffocation and not a bed to be had in the place.

'There'd been a small National Hunt meeting there that day, to be continued on the day following, and the place was full of bookies and jockeys and stable-hands, and the sort of crowd that one always finds in a place on such an occasion. Those were the days before everybody owned a car and congestions of that sort were more frequent and denser than they are today.

'We were too dog-tired to go any farther, and we soon found that there wasn't any sort of cottage that could take us in, so Paston said we'd have to bivouac in the Lodge, after all. There was no caretaker there, but an old woman who'd been a servant in his grandfather's family, and who lodged with her son's family in a cottage somewhere handy, had the keys and went in occasionally to clean out the place.

'We found out where she lived and went to get the keys from her. She didn't know Paston at first, because she hadn't seen him since he was a kid, but directly he established his identity she was all over him. But when he talked of camping out for the night in the Lodge, as his place was called, her eyes began to stand out of her head.

' "Have you forgotten what night it is?" she asked, in a whisper. "It's the fourth of April. You'd better sleep anywhere than there tonight. The 'Gamblers' will get one of you."

'We both thought at first that she was referring to the village being thronged with the lesser lights of the racing world. I agreed that it was the fourth of April and not the first. And Paston pointed out to her in the weary, supercilious voice he used then that we had nowhere else to go; but for all that we had the devil of a job to get the keys out of her.

'She worked herself up into a pretty dangerous state of excitement and said we were to have her bed instead—anything rather than that we were to sleep in that house. We couldn't extract from her the precise cause of her trepidation, for she was a bit incoherent, but we gathered that the Lodge was haunted, that the night of the fourth of April was the time when things happened, and that if we stayed there the Gamblers would assuredly get one of us.

'We were both amused. Paston pointed out, in his quiet, bored way, that these Gamblers— whoever they were—had left his grandfather alone. He remembered afterwards that his grandfather only used to spend odd weeks there during the hunting season, which was well over by the beginning of April. Anyhow, we got the keys at last from the old lady's daughter-in-law, from whom we also borrowed a couple of blankets, and when we went away the old lady herself stood screaming warnings at us.

'I may as well say here and now that I never discovered what legend—and I suppose there must have been one—was attached to the house. Something more than curiosity took me back to that part of the world a year or two later, but the old woman had died in the meantime, and nobody else in the neighbourhood seemed to know anything about it.

'As we set forth together through the dusk Paston remarked that he didn't altogether disbelieve in haunted houses. He wanted first-hand evidence, he said, and psychic research was one of the sciences he intended dipping into. But we both agreed that we were far too tired to make any investigations that night.

'The house was about a quarter of a mile from the village. Paston pushed open an iron gate and led the way up a short drive which curved between evergreens. I remember that we stood under a bit of a porch while I lit a candle, and Paston opened with one of the keys an old door with a segment-shaped fanlight over the top.

' "We'd better camp out in the dining-room," Paston said. "It was always considered the warmest room in the house."

'So I followed him into a room on the left of the hall, which was small and square and panelled. For the warmest room in the house we found it pretty dam cold with our one blanket each—we weren't old campaigners then—and we settled down in opposite comers, still wearing most of our clothes. But we were so leg-weary that we could have slept on a clothes-line. I was asleep within three minutes, and I don't know the precise time when I awoke.

'I came out of sleep for all the world as if I were recovering from a drug. I was conscious of being awake long before I opened my eyes, but I hadn't half the use of my faculties. As soon as I did open my eyes I was aware that the room, which had been quite bare when we turned in, was furnished and dimly illumined. This didn't astonish me for I was still so much asleep—if not actually dreaming—that I wasn't at first capable of being surprised at anything.

'I can't describe how the room was furnished, save that there was a table in the middle, for my gaze was concentrated in that direction. I was only just vaguely aware of other parts of the room. On this table were four candles in metal sticks burning low and bluish, and around the table were seated four men who were playing cards. Three of them were dressed in the fashion of nearly two hundred years ago, and the fourth, collarless, as if he had just jumped up from his blanket on the floor to join them, was Paston.

'You'll at once suggest that I was dreaming. The thought occurred to me then and there, and I raised myself on an elbow, expecting to see the whole scene suddenly melt. Then the terror of a nightmare overcame me as I saw the faces of Paston's three companions. It would be unfair to humanity to call them human faces, but for sheer poverty of words I suppose I must call them that. All three were Vice incarnate. I have been to nearly all the picture galleries in Europe, but no artist in depicting devils has ever succeeded in conveying to canvas anything a tithe so abominable.

'I could not, of course, see the faces of all four at once. One had his back to me, but as he turned his head to left or right to follow the play of the cards, I saw his profile, and it was all I wanted to see. But the face that shocked me most was Paston's, for a more disagreeable transfiguration it would be impossible to imagine.

'Everything transpired in silence. Not a word was spoken, nor did I hear the movement of a chair, the rustle of clothes, nor the chink of the gold pieces as they were passed. It was as if I were stone deaf or watching a drama of the cinema. I don't know what game they were playing, but it was a quick game, a mere matter of dealing and showing the cards. And Paston was winning heavily.

'The table just in front of him was piled high with gold pieces, and as I watched he won more and more from the dwindling stores of the other three. I've said his face was changed. There was greed and triumph in his eyes, and on his lips the grin of a man who isn't quite master of his emotions when his luck is well in. Knowing Paston as I did, it increased the horror of the situation a thousandfold to see him thus. Look into his face today and you'll catch a glimpse of what I saw in it then.

'As I crouched there I fought hard to believe it was a dream, and told myself that if I slewed my head round and looked into the comer in which Paston settled down for the night I should see him lying there asleep; but I found that I couldn't move my head. I simply just had to watch, and I saw Paston at the table triumphantly showing hand after hand, and drawing in the money pushed across to him. It was like watching three crooks encouraging their victim before settling to the task of robbing him.

'I tried to cry out to Paston and warn him, but my tongue seemed to fill my mouth. How long I was compelled to watch I don't know, before I felt unconsciousness stealing over me again. This was a beastly sensation, like fainting, and I tried to fight against it, but I had to go.

'When I woke up broad sunlight was pouring in through the windows, and I was relieved to see that the room was as bare as it had been when we went to bed, and Paston still sound asleep in the opposite comer.

'I felt pretty cheap, for all the world as if I'd done myself too well overnight. Even then I couldn't quite persuade myself that I had been dreaming when I saw what I saw. It was all too vivid for a dream, I thought. And I had a horror of that house, even now that the floor of the room was dabbled with sunlight, and I wanted to clear out then and there. So I woke old Paston.

'I was particular to ask Paston if he'd dreamed anything. He said he couldn't remember, but supposed he had, as he felt washed-out. He'd got himself over-tired, he said, and must have slept too heavily, so sleep hadn't done him any good.

' "You didn't see any ghosts, I suppose?" he asked lightly, a little later, while we were both putting on our shoes.

'I told him No. I wasn't going to tell him. Why should I? But I asked him if he remembered hearing anything of the story of the old woman had tried to tell us.

'He shook his head.

' "All quite new to me. I dare say we slept too soundly to give a chance to any spirits who may have wanted to manifest themselves. But I seem to remember years ago hearing that this room was called the Gamblers' Room. That may have been a sort of family joke, because my grandfather was fond of playing whist for small stakes. Or it may go farther back and have something to do with the old lady's ghost story."

'He wanted to show me all over the premises, but I'd had enough of the house, and I managed to drag him away. And even then, when we'd bathed and had a sort of breakfast at the inn he didn't want to leave Great Chowney. It was the second day of the local races, and, to my astonishment—and trouble—I found that he wanted to go.

' "My dear chap," I said, "I didn't think that sort of thing was much in your line."

' "Nor is it," he answered. "Of course, I haven't the least intention of betting. But I've never been to a race-meeting, and I thought it would be a good opportunity of seeing some of the queer types you find at such places."

'I didn't like the sound of this, and I managed to head him off, although I would have rather liked to go myself And that was the beginning of the new Paston.

'From that morning I began to see subtle changes in him. I tried to persuade myself that they existed only in my imagination, but the harder I tried the more certain I became that the man had really entered upon a new phase. The old subjects of talk ceased to interest him. He answered questions absently, and had fits of moroseness. He was like that all through our last term at Cambridge, and although we were in College I didn't see so much of him. But I saw the gradual changes, and so did others. A lot of other men of our year, of the more gamesome sort, who'd known him all the time, actually thought he'd improved. I knew otherwise.

'If what I saw wasn't a dream—and I firmly believe it wasn't—and if he actually sat and played with those three Horrors, he knew nothing about it afterwards. He doesn't know a word of it today. But they'd inoculated him with the virus of gambling and for a year after we came down I saw the poison slowly working in him.

'You know most of the rest. Money went through his hands like water.

"Four Monkey" Paston the men on the rails used to call him. He's reduced mostly to the Silver Ring now, and the knowledgeable sort point him out as having been in his day one of the heaviest plungers of recent years. He's learned his lesson, but even now he can't keep away. If he were starving he'd gamble with another beggar for crusts.

'His people haven't altogether chucked him, although they know he's hopeless. There's a bit of a family fund for him, and he gets little doles dribbled out regularly. Knowing what I know I can't help feeling sorry for the poor devil. I firmly believe that something stronger than himself got hold of him—some evil stronger than human nature could withstand. And when I see him I think, "There but for the grace of God goes Francis Storman."

'I'm glad I've told you; not that there's much chance of your believing me. At least it's an explanation of some sort. And if you look back and remember the Paston you used to know as a youngster I defy you to think of any other explanation, reasonable or not, which would bear psychological examination. He—Hallo!'

Storman's narrative came thus very abruptly to an end. He beckoned to the man who had just shouldered his way through the swing door.

'Here we are, Paston—over here.'

Paston came over smiling, his eyes aflame with excitement.

'Dim Star,' he whispered hoarsely, 'is out in the three o'clock tomorrow. They think he's got a stone in hand. I expect they'll back it away from the course, and it'll come back on the Blower. But we ought to get a good price when the market opens. Look here, Storman, I'm not quite a pauper. There's a shot or two left in the locker, but a cousin of mine's got power of attorney for me. I shall have some money in a few days, but I want to have a good win over Dim Star tomorrow. So, if you wouldn't mind lending me'

Did I believe Storman's story? How could I? And yet leaning over the table before me was this unsavoury slave of a besetting sin, while there dwelt in my memory a boy on the verge of manhood who had been almost too immune from even the most amiable faults.

Whenever I think of the tale Storman told me I remember that boy and set his figure side by side with my more recent memory of the man—the broken man with his racing jargon, his shameless seediness, his air of having completely gone under—and I can find no human reason to account for the change.

Do I believe Storman's story? Well, I wonder.

A.M. Burrage – The Life And Times.

Alfred McLelland Burrage, better known as simply AM Burrage, was born in Hillingdon, Middlesex on July 1st, 1889, to Alfred Sherrington Burrage and Mary E. Burrage. On his Father's side writing already ran in the family's blood as both he and an uncle, Edwin Harcourt Burrage, were writers of the then very popular boys' magazine fiction.

Life in late Victorian times was by no means easy and writing has always been a precarious career for most. For an insight into the young AM and his surroundings it is interesting to see how certain facts were captured in the 1891 census when he was aged one. The family is listed as living at Uxbridge Common in Hillingdon. His father is 40 and his mother 36. In the next census of 1901, and with it the end of the Victorian era, the family has moved to 1 Park Villa, Newbury. In that time his father has aged 17 years his mother 6 years and young AM has disappeared from the records. It's almost a precursor to one of his stories.

There is little documented about his growing up and education. What we can glean though is something about his environment. His neighbours were varied: a tailor's journeyman, a corn porter, a lodging-house keeper and a grocer's assistant. Nothing particularly illustrious, so times cannot have been as rosy as they should, especially in the light of his Father's hard work. Alfred Sherrington wrote for The Boy's World, Our Boys' Paper, The Boys of England,

and various others. He also appears to have written under the pseudonym Philander Jackson and edited The Boys' Standard and that one of his more celebrated pieces was a retelling of the story of Sweeney Todd entitled "The String of Peals; or, Passages from the Life of Sweeney Todd, the Demon Barber".

Sadly Alfred Sherrington Burrage died in 1906. There is a biographical note in Lloyd's Magazine, from 1921, which suggests that young Alfred McLelland was studying at St. Augustine's, the Catholic Foundation School in Ramsgate, and most probably away from home at the time.

A.M. Burrage was 16 years old when he had his first story published; the same year as his father's death, in the prestigious boys' paper, Chums. It was a great start to his professional career and whether doors had been opened by his father and family or not the young man's career now had to stand on its own. He was now primary provider for the household and this was the only way he could do it. His Mother, sister and aunt must be provided for.

Magazine fiction was his family's blood and business and for A. M. Burrage, business was good. He established himself as a competent and creative writer and was busy writing stories and articles on a weekly basis for publications such as Boys' Friend Weekly, Boys' Herald, Comic Life, Vanguard, Dreadnought, Triumph Library Cheer Boys Cheer, and Gem, under the pseudonym 'Cooee'.

However, unlike his father and uncle who had remained firmly and easily categorised as boys' writers, he had his sights set on the more well regarded, more lucrative, adult market. Burrage was aided in his early years as a professional writer by Isobel Thorne of the off-Fleet Street publishing firm Shurey's. Her publications have been characterised as "low in price, modest in payments, but whose readers were avid for romance, thrills, sensation, strong characterisation and neat plotting", and this estimation of her publications also fits nicely the description of Burrage's own writing at that time. For a young writer this sort of readership was vital, and the modest wages he received were bolstered by the exposure the publications brought him. Burrage was certainly helped by Thorne's use of young writers.

At the time Burrage was beginning to really establish himself as a writer, the entire magazine fiction scene was benefiting from what we would now see as disruptive influences: new printing techniques, a growing readership with more disposable income and leisure time and other media failing to provide – though obviously movies and such were only in their infancy at the time. The market was lively and commercial, and the readership interested, excitable and willing to pay. P. G. Wodehouse, of Jeeves fame, recalls these years:

We might get turned down by the Strand, but there was always the hope of landing with Nash's, the Story-teller, the London, the Royal, the Red, the Yellow, Cassell's, the New, the Novel, the Grand, the Pall Mall, and the Windsor, not to mention Blackwood's, Cornhill, Chambers's and probably about a dozen more I've forgotten.

With War clouds darkening the skies of Europe in 1914 Burrage was firmly established as a magazine writer, securing publication in London Magazine and The Storyteller, which were both highly prestigious publications. Alongside he had plenty printed in less illustrious publications such as Short Stories Illustrated.

By now Burrage, a young man of twenty-four-year-was eligible for the Armed Services. Under the 'Derby Scheme' he confirmed that he was available for service if called upon in December 1915. Conscription was to follow shortly though, by that time, Burrage had already voluntarily enrolled in the Artists Rifles.

The significance of Burrage's decision to join the Artists Rifles is made clear by the nature of the unit itself. They formed in the middle of the nineteenth century, a group of volunteer artists comprising musicians, writers, painters and engravers. Minerva and Mars were their patrons, one of wisdom, arts, and defence, the other of war. The unit boasted several significant figures as ex-servicemen, including Dante Gabriel Rossetti, Algernon Charles Swinburne and William Morris. It was a popular unit with students and recent postgraduates, and the training was considered and extensive.

In Burrage's vivid, celebrated account of World War I entitled War is War, he insists that he was a volunteer and not a conscript, though as has already been noted, it is quite possible that his decision to join such a respected territorial unit may have been more of an effort to secure himself a more congenial army posting; had he waited for conscription, he would have had little choice over those with whom he was posted. Unlike poets Wilfred Owen or Edward Thomas, Burrage did not achieve a commission, and he suggests in War is War that this may be a result of his extremely unmilitary personality and his shortcomings as a soldier.

Add to this the fact that as the breadwinner for the family he was putting himself in harm's way. If anything were to happen to him the result on the family would be devastating. With the death of
Edwin Harcourt Burrage in 1916 it came even more starkly into focus.

Even though he was now a soldier he was still a writer and writers had to write. It also helped that it was a distraction from the mindless carnage around him. He experimented with various genres, excelling in the one that was to prove most lucrative for him; the light romance, in which a male character invariably meets a female character, there is a problem or hurdle to their being together, they overcome it and they live happily ever after. Burrage's talent for this formula was such that he could work seemingly endless minor variations from the same basic storyline and so he was able to keep writing a steady body of easy work.

He gives a fascinating account of the practicalities of writing such fiction during wartime in War is War, in which he remarks on the difficulties of censorship: "the problem of censorship was an acute one to me. It was well enough to write a story, but the difficulty was to get it censored. Officers were shy of tackling five thousand words or so, written in indelible pencil..." After some time he managed to find a chaplain who was willing to undertake the censorship. However, in order to secure this chaplain's favour and thus his services he was obliged to appear to be holy. Though he did so in earnest while he was with the chaplain, his efforts were dashed when the chaplain found him, sprawled on top of a young girl, and realised Burrage's piety to be a fraudulent con. As Burrage had anticipated, the reality of his behaviour ensured that this particular opportunity was swiftly ended. Resourceful to the last, though, he writes of his solution: "there were 'green envelopes' which could be sent away sealed and were liable only to censorship at the base, but these were only sparingly issued... I met an A.S.C. lorry driver who had stolen enough green envelopes to last me for the rest of the war; and since he only wanted two francs for them I was free of the censorship from that day forward."

Although we know that Burrage had his family to support at home as an incentive to keep writing, at times in War is War he reveals a more intimate aspect of his relationship with his work.

"It was a great relief to me to write when it was at all possible – to sit down and lose myself in that pleasant old world I used to know and pretend to myself that there never had been a war. Some of my editors seemed of the opinion that we were not suffering from one now. One used to write to me saying "Couldn't you let me have one of your light, charming love stories of country house life by next Thursday." I would get these letters in the trenches during the usual 'morning hate' when my fingers were too numb to hold a pencil, when I was worn out with work and sleeplessness, and when I was extremely doubtful if there ever would be another Thursday".

Writing is a useful therapy and for Burrage it provided a means to escape if only for a short time to a world that he could control and move at will. With the misery and harsh conditions of the War dragging on he was eventually invalided and so he returned to England.

One of the best insights we have as to the character which Burrage presented on his return from the war is to be found in Lloyd's's 1920 publication of Captain Dorry, one of Burrage's story series. In that publication there was included a brief sketch of Burrage, describing his personality.

A.M. BURRAGE is the type of young man who might very well walk out of one of his own stories. He commenced yarn-spinning as a boy of fifteen at St Augustine's, Ramsgate, writing stories of school life to provide himself with pocket-money. Since then he has won his spurs as one of the most popular of magazine writers. Everything he does has charm and reflects his own romantic spirit – for he is incurably romantic and hopelessly lazy. It is his misfortune, although he would not admit it, that his work finds a too ready market. Nevertheless, his friends hope that one day he will wake up and do justice to himself. Otherwise he may end up as a "best-seller", a fate which doubtless he contemplates with equanimity.

Despite the sketch's fairly accurate but negative summation of Burrage's literary output up to that point, some of his stories seem to exhibit a desire to write about more than just his usual romantic plots. The most immediate change of this nature is in his decision to bring some of his wartime experience into his work, despite being perfectly aware that such writing was not at all what his editors desired, for they feared it would upset and intimidate their readership.

An example of this can be found in "A Town of Memories", published in 1919 in Grand Magazine, in which he uses his well rehearsed romantic story with a slight shift of emphasis to explore his own return from the war and the general reception which soldiers received on their return. Following a young officer as he returns to the town in which he grew up, Burrage portrays an almost hostile environment into which he returns; he is unrecognised, and nobody pays any interest, respect or attention to him or his stories of the war, nor even to his reception of the Distinguished Service Order. Instead, the people of the town have their own interests and priorities with which to concern themselves. Though this contentious portrayal of post-war society certainly marks a slight shift in Burrage's writing, he returns to the romantic convention expected of him by reuniting the officer with a beautiful girl who had admired him throughout school. It would be harsh to not accept that market conditions expected one thing and to ignore them would mean turning his back on publications who still clamoured for his penmanship.

Another of Burrage's alternative directions is to be found in "The Recurring Tragedy", in which a General whose war tactics of attrition had been to the slaughtered cost of his soldiers, and he comes to re-imagine his own past as a Judas figure in a terrible vision. The Strange Career of Captain Dorry became a series for Lloyd's Magazine in 1920 about a gentleman crook and an ex-officer with a Military Cross who, idle in peacetime, meets a mysterious man called Fewgin whose business is in stolen goods and mind reading. Fewgin realises Dorry is a suitable candidate for recruitment into his gang of like-minded ex-military thieves, stealing only from "certain vampires who made money out of the war, and, by keeping up prices, are continuing to make money out of the peace". Again, in this motive, we see a glimpse of Burrage's own feelings on the war, as there is undoubtedly a bitterness towards those profiting from the suffering of others in such a manner. Fewgin justifies himself, saying:

"I help brave men who cannot help themselves. I give them a chance to get back a little of their own from the men who battened and fattened on them, who helped to starve their dependents while they were fighting, who smoked fat cigars in the haunts of their betters, and hoped the war might never end."

Burrage began to see slightly more success in the 1920s, achieving a couple of hard back publications entitled Some Ghost Stories and Poor Dear Esme. The latter, a comedy, concerns a boy who, for various reasons, is forced to disguise himself as a girl. Though these hard cover publications were a notable achievement, and one of which he was proud, the fact was that there was less money in it than in the magazines. In his history of the Strand Magazine, Reginald Pound portrays Burrage around this time, likening him to his equally prolific contemporary Herbert Shaw, considering them "two Bohemian temperaments that suffused and at times confused gifts from which more was expected than come forth. They had a precise knowledge of the popular short story as the product of calculated design. Both privately despised it, though it was their living."

The early 1920s, and with them a boom in prosperity, hope and happiness, now brought with them an increase in demand for war stories. Rather than preferring to ignore the atrocities of the war, which had seemed the general attitude in the immediate post-war years, society became more interested and concerned with the manner in which the war was fought, and the greed and political battles which had necessitated such bloodshed. Burrage answered this demand in 1930 with his own epochal piece, War Is War. He published under the pseudonym 'Ex-Private X', saying "were it otherwise I could not tell the truth about myself", though its publisher, Victor Gollancz, "who published the book and greatly admired it, had to point out that the critics would hardly take the book seriously if it became known that the author earned his living producing two or three slushy love stories a week".

In one of a series of letters he wrote to his contemporary and fellow writer Dorothy Sayers, Burrage bemoans how War is War "promised to be a great success, but was only a moderate one". The book itself was received with reviews on both sides of the spectrum. Cyril Fall's War Books, a survey of post-war writing published in 1930, gives a clear indication as to why the critics were so mixed in reception of the book. He writes:

This book is extremely uneven in quality. The account of the attack at Paschendaele and of conditions at Cambrai after the great German counter-attack are very good indeed; in fact among the best of their kind. But the rest is disfigured by an unreasoned and unpleasant attack on superiors and all troops other than those of the front line, which is all the more astonishing because the author is inclined to harp upon his social position as compared with that of many of the officers with whom he came in contact. He does not use as much bad language as many writers on the War, but his methods of abuse will leave on some of his readers at least a worse impression than the most highly-spiced language.

Dorothy Sayers was the editor at Victor Gollanz for anthologies of ghost and horror stories which included stories by Burrage. She says, in one of her letters of Burrage's story The Waxwork, a piece beyond the nerves of the editors, "what you say about "The Waxwork" sounds very exciting, just the sort of thing I want. Our nerves are stronger than those of the editors of periodicals, and we will publish anything, so long as it does not bring us into conflict with the Home Secretary". Though their correspondence began as strictly business, Burrage's acquaintance with Atherton Fleming, Sayers's husband, allowed their interactions to become less formal and friendlier. Burrage wrote of Fleming "I hope to encounter him soon in one of the Fleet Street tea-shops". 'Tea-shop' being a popular euphemism for the pub, where both Burrage and Fleming could frequently be found, though their alcohol consumption came to damage both their health and their professions, with Burrage coming off the worse.

Happily for Burrage, as a result of being featured in one of Sayers's anthologies, The Waxwork became one of his best-known stories and it would grab the attention of the film companies several times down the years even becoming an episode in the TV series 'Alfred Hitchcock Presents'.

The developing friendship between Burrage and Sayers enabled him to reveal more details of his personal life, admitting to her his "neuritis at both ends (legs and eyes)", and hinting at his troubles with alcohol: "Fleet Street is not a good place for a man who delights in succumbing to temptation, and whose doctor says that even small doses of alcohol are poison to him". Sayers sympathises, replying that Fleming "agrees with you entirely about the temptations of Fleet Street; he has, however, succeeded, through sheer strength of character, in being able to drink soda-water in the face of all his fellow journalists".

In another of Burrage's letters, he apologises for a delay in sending proofs of a story, with the words:

I have had a pretty thin time lately through illness and anxiety. And for days on end haven't had the energy in me to write a letter, and when I had the energy to send a complete set of proofs to you I found I hadn't the postage money (This is when you take out your handkerchief and start sobbing). I owed my late agent over £1000, so I got practically nothing out of War is War. He stuck to it. Well, he is paid off now, and so are my arrears of income tax. All this took a toll of my very small earning capacity, and I have been sold up. This on top of something which promised to be a great success and was only a moderate one, was a bit too much for me. Still, in spite of sickness I am resilient and shall float again. "You can't keep a good man down," as the whale said about Jonah.

For a man who had so many stories in so many magazines, and was gaining pace in Sayers's anthologies as a talented writer of horror stories, his income will have been far higher than the then average wage, and yet as he says, he finds himself short of money.

Several questions are left unanswered about his personal life. It is unclear whether he was still supporting family, or whether he spent the majority of his money on alcohol, or whether he chose to conceal his true fortunes from those around him. Perhaps most incongruous is the apparent absence of a wife; though his death certificate indicates that he had one, listed as H.A. Burrage, he seems never to mention her to Sayers.

He was around forty-two when he wrote that apology letter to Sayers, though in tone and circumstance it seems to be from a man in a far later stage of his life.

Burrage continued writing until his death in 1956, and continued to be prolifically published. Indeed, the Evening News alone published some forty of his stories between 1950-56. His death is recorded at Edgware General Hospital on 18th December, and the causes of his death are recorded as congestive cardiac failure, arteriosclerosis and chronic bronchitis. He was sixty-seven years old, and his last address is listed as 105 Vaughan Road, Harrow.

Though his name is not often remembered in lists of prominent writers of his time, or even it's genres, his ghost stories are highly regarded by critics and fans alike, while his life story tells us much about the trials and stresses placed on authors during and after the war, and on soldiers returning from that war. His reluctant acceptance that the money was in the magazines while the esteem was in the poorly-paying hard covers, and his persistence as a writer, speak of a determined man, doomed to circumstance yet living as best he could.

In ending A.M Burrage wrote a few sentences which best sum up two things. Firstly his love for his son Simon (who sadly passed away in October 2013 and was a great and passionate advocate for his Father's works.) and secondly his succinct reasons for writing.

TO JULIAN SIMON FIELD BURRAGE

who at the moment of writing will
soon achieve the great age of four.
From somebody who loves him.

In War is War I admitted being a professional writer, or in other words one who depends for his bread and cheese and beer on writing, typing or dictating strings of sentences which his masters, the Public, are kind enough to buy and presumably to read.

The book brought me letters from a few old friends and a great many new ones. A large percentage of the new friends, who missed having seen that my identity was rather unkindly betrayed by the Press, wrote and asked (a) who I was and (b) what sort of stories did I write?

The answer to the second question will be found in the following pages. The answer to the first question is 'Nobody Much', worse luck.

Most of these stories were written with the intention of giving the reader a pleasant shudder, in the hope that he will take a lighted candle to bed with him—for candle-makers must be considered in these hard times. Some have already made their bow from the pages of the monthly magazines. The best have, quite naturally, been rejected.

www.ingramcontent.com/pod-product-compliance
Lightning Source LLC
Chambersburg PA
CBHW060132260626
47160CB00005B/2083